VEGAS DESTINY

A novel by

Barbara Maines

PublishAmerica
Baltimore

© 2007 by Barbara Maines.
All rights reserved. No part of this book may be reproduced, stored in a retrieval system or transmitted in any form or by any means without the prior written permission of the publishers, except by a reviewer who may quote brief passages in a review to be printed in a newspaper, magazine or journal.

All characters in this book are fictitious, and any resemblance to real persons, living or dead, is coincidental.

First printing

At the specific preference of the author, PublishAmerica allowed this work to remain exactly as the author intended, verbatim, without editorial input.

Hardcover 9781462619382
Softcover 1424175232
PUBLISHED BY PUBLISHAMERICA, LLLP
www.publishamerica.com
Baltimore

Printed in the United States of America

DEDICATED TO THE MEMORY OF

DWIGHT DAVID

With all my love and eternal Regret

Mother

CHAPTERS

The Baby	7
Jimmy Notman	21
Survival Lessons	29
The Back-Up Man	35
Vegas Honeymoon	39
Last Will and Testament	43
Yours, Mine and Ours	46
Vegas Anniversary	51
Condolences	57
Revenge	63
Sid	69
The New Employee	75
Queenie	77
First Snow	83
And They Came	89
The Change	93
The Catch	97
A Call For Help	101
The Real Reason	105
Wedding Plans	107
The Easy Way?	109
Another Wrong One, God	117
Hello Generation Six	121
The Big Flood	125
The Myers' Curse	131
Return to Vegas	135
Of Course He's A Man	143
Mr. Hamilton	149
The Widow Hamilton	153
The Last Goodbye	157
And The Rains Came	159

For They Will See God	163
Prayers	169
Katrina-Past Hell	173
Rita-The Uninvited Guest That Stayed	177
Final Visit	181
The End?	185

CHAPTER ONE

THE BABY

Bobby pulled back the wooden slats of the shutters in the Elephant House and peered out over the river. It was early morning and the Tickfaw looked like an angry, determined woman, pushing everything out of its way in an attempt to reach the gulf. Bounding and cascading over upturned trees left by the hurricanes, it looked gray and vicious.

When the trees wouldn't move, the water never stopped grinding away at the wooden barricades, attempting to pulverize them with forceful battering. Then the Tickfaw would build up white piles of foam as if it were an animal going mad.

She knew this would be her last home. When she and Clark built it here on the banks of the Tickfaw River, she named it her Elephant House. Hopefully, it would be her last home, the place where she would die, in spite of her pact with the Devil and the Vegas death curse.

"Why didn't you tell me what you meant when you named it the Elephant House?' Linda asked, almost panicky. That Christmas her younger sister had given her a large, obviously very expensive, elephant coffee table—along with many smaller elephant gifts. "I don't want to even think about you dying, and I would never have given you even one damned elephant if I had known why you called it that name. Elephants are for good luck."

"Well, if I have the good luck to die here instead of Vegas, I shall be the happiest corpse ever," she informed her sister, without explaining the reason for her statement.

It hadn't taken death long to visit the Elephant House, after that conversation.

As Bobby stood there watching the river, she wondered if she would ever come to terms with God and her old friend, the Devil. She wondered when did it all begin, but in her heart she could pinpoint the exact day, that day when she was sixteen, sitting in a bathtub...

She languished in the bathtub, admiring her toes, lifting one at a time, watching the water slowly drip back down into the tub. They were really pretty toes; little, square and very clean. She could remember a few years ago when she was younger and they weren't so clean. She could still feel the sticky gray and white chicken goo squashed between them when she visited her Grandpa B.T.'s farm.

In the afternoons Bobby sat in Grandpa B.T.'s soft lap, listening to the ballgame playing from the radio sitting on the kitchen table. "Strike one, strike two, there's a foul ball to the upper stand. The runner on third—he's making a dash for home plate!"

With her right thumb in her mouth, and her left arm up and over the top of her head holding onto her right ear, she cuddled into his lap. It was perfect childhood bliss. To this day that ear stuck out like Prince Charles ears and her front teeth were bowed out, like a misshaped miniature Roman coliseum.

B.T. birthed her in that very farmhouse in Deerfield, Ohio before the doctor arrived. It was an unexpected arrival when Margaret told him the baby was coming. In his excitement, he mistakenly thought the baby was a boy and said, "Well, look at that cute little 'bobby'."

Upon closer inspection he exclaimed, "Whoops, he doesn't have a bobby!"

Margaret, still weak from the delivery, nevertheless gave a little laugh and said, "Pop, that will be its name, whether it turns out to be a boy or girl, that's it. Now, check real close, does it have a bobby, or not. Do I have a boy or girl?"

So that's the reason she had a boy's name. In some families only recipes and pictures are passed from one generation to the next. In the Myers' family the story of Bobby's birth became infamous, along with the family tradition of calling their penises bobby, springing from the moment B.T. thought he delivered a baby boy. Within a couple generations no one remembered exactly why the young men in the family referred to their most precious part as a bobby, or why the women picked up that pet name for their husbands' penis, that's just the way it was, as traditional as the family apple pie recipe.

Today, as she lay in that big white bathtub remembering the old farm days, she could smell the lilacs in bloom right outside the open bathroom window. Ohio was experiencing its first sweet-smelling, sparkling spring day on the other side of that window.

She could spend hours in the tub. Daddy always bragged his bathtub was as big as a swimming pool, and it was. In the 1940's in rural Ohio a big bathtub was a luxury and Bobby was sitting in this big luxury.

But today there was a nagging thing in the back of her mind.

Last night Jimmy mentioned again about joining the Navy right after his graduation, barely a month away. Oh well, she would become like that girl Grandma Milton was reading about. What was her name?...let's see...Scarlett. Yes, that's it, Scarlett. She, Bobby, would be just like Scarlett, she would just think about it tomorrow. Grandma told her all about Scarlett. Grandma laughed and said, "If only Scarlett could see Atlanta today." Her daddy's mama, who lived right next door across the driveway, who painted pretty pictures, who sometimes told delightful little naughty stories, and who was always there to listen to her stories.

Mama always referred to her as Lyle's mother. Not once had she ever heard Mama call Grandma Milton by any other name, it was always Lyle's mother, spoken with an attitude.

Mama called Daddy's sisters names sometimes, but their real names were Harriet and Lucille, and whenever Bobby wanted to visit these two aunties in Cleveland, Bobby could hear loud arguments between her parents.

Mama objected.

Sometimes Daddy won the argument and she was off to spend a glorious time on the streets in Cleveland. Auntie Harriet permitted her complete freedom: she could hop buses, roller skate on East 9th Street, right past the Roxy Theatre, the infamous burlesque theatre, and swim in front of the reflection pool of City Hall. Mama would be horrified if she knew.

She could stand there in Auntie Harriet's apartment and look right through the dirt-encrusted window of the Cleveland Morgue. And watch. In that same filthy apartment, she would turn out the lights and then switch them on again and there were cockroaches—everywhere—all over everything.

Every window sill was blackened with soot brought up by the wind coming from the industrial section, called the flats, which belched out dirty smoke, day after day. Over the entire city tens of thousands windowsills remained gritty with black soot, no matter if they were wiped clean daily. Auntie Harriet never bothered to ever wipe her sills, or scrub the floors, or kill the cockroaches. But Bobby thought none of that was important, because she knew Auntie Harriet loved her…

At that very moment the bathroom door flew open. She lay there naked, exposed, a body-shy sixteen-year old, with Mama standing over her.

"I think you're pregnant, you haven't had a period this month. How long has this been going on? What will people say?" accused Mama.

No time to grab a towel, nothing to hide behind, she made a feeble attempt to reach the towel, and there was Mama scrutinizing her, taking in every inch of the naked body. No one, not Mama, Jimmy or even her best friend Lois, had ever seen that completely disrobed, teenaged body.

She was humiliated.

Then an angry, persistent Margaret reached down and yanked the defenseless uncovered sixteen-year old body out of that safe tub and demanded an answer.

It was a bizarre teenage scene Bobby always remembered with embarrassment, then two days later another scene remained horribly embedded in Bobby's memory.

"My God, Marge, this has to stop, you're killing her!" Bobby heard her daddy above the ringing in her head as he stepped over her, lying on the kitchen floor. Daddy had this habit of running his hands through his hair when he was worried, and she could see him reach up and fingercomb his hair as he pleaded with Marge to stop. Mama put something in a glass of orange juice, telling her to drink it, and now Daddy sounded like he was in a cavern somewhere—only she knew he just stepped over her, as he pleaded with Mama to stop.

Finally, when nothing worked to bring about her monthly period, Margaret marched her to Dr. Johns who verified, indeed, Bobby was pregnant.

The little quickly-arranged country wedding was rather nice. A consoling Preacher Knipe said that when two people married young they often began to look like each other after twenty-five or fifty years. Mama made her a new dress to wear for the occasion, a demure white pique blouse with an aqua blue skirt, and she asked her best friend, Lois, to be her Maid of Honor. Someone thoughtfully filmed the entire ceremony.

Tab Hunter handsome, a young Jimmy, resigned to the fate of being a reluctant bridegroom, rigidly stood in his only suit looking every bit the man when someone pointed out, "At least he graduated from high school."

"Are you sorry?" he whispered, after they both said "I do". Bobby shook her head no, but inside she felt like she was still sitting buck-naked in that sparkling big white bathtub.

"Well, I am," he unexpectedly confessed.

She would never forget that date: June 4, 1947.

Jimmy moved in and shared Bobby's small bedroom on the second floor of the farmhouse in Blackhorse, Ohio. They slept in the bed where she had lost her virginity to him while her parents were at a Halloween party. That October night, eight months ago, she took her bloodstained sheet and hid it in the back of her closet.

"Bobby, what's this doing here?" Margaret yanked the soiled sheet from the back of the closet.

"Golly, Mama, don't I have aneeee privacy?" Bobby whined. She knew the answer, and sent up a little prayer that Mama wouldn't demand an explanation. Bobby pretended to go back to sleep. How could she explain a blood-stained sheet in the middle of the month? Play dumb, perhaps Mama would think it had been there for a couple weeks, since her last period.

Maybe Margaret was afraid to delve too deeply for a response to her question about the bloody sheet. She hesitated, and then quickly scooped up the sheet. Tossing it into her laundry basket, she quickly left the room and headed for the basement, two flights down.

"Well, my shoulders are broad," Margaret said to herself, as she stomped down the basement stairs. "Let her accuse me of snooping, at least I will know what she's doing, it's my job to keep her safe. Lyle lets her go visit Harriet in Cleveland, awful filthy woman, in that filthy apartment. And she goes over and cries on Lyle's mother's shoulders. If she goes bad, what will people say? Well, I won't let her get in trouble. My daughter is going to college, Oberlin College, where there is a great music department. She's going to become a concert pianist, have a career, be somebody, and do big things."

Last night Lyle accused her, "Marge, you wouldn't be happy if I gave you the moon made of green cheese with a fence around it."

Now where on earth do you suppose he picked that one up? Well, her daughter was going to be the best, she was going to be educated like her family, not like Lyle's family and those dirty, immoral sisters of his, always getting married and divorced. And all those men, Margaret shuddered...pigs, both of them.

At the same time Margaret was analyzing the virtues of Lyle's sisters, Bobby sat in her private world, her bedroom. Often as years went by she wished she could barge in and ask the new owners of that house if she could just visit there and spend a few hours.

Mama wallpapered it in a small blue and white flowered print, and somewhere her parents found a little curved vanity stand. Mama made a filmy, gauzy gathered skirt for it, held fast with thumbtacks. The little drawer in the front held her diary and other precious objects, and she kept the diary key taped to the bottom of the drawer. She was painfully aware Mama snooped in her things and read all her mail.

The room, with its low ceilings situated under the sloped roof, was the only place in the whole wide world, besides Aunt Harriet's house, where she was really happy, away from Mama's vigilant and suspicious eyes.

She even loved the closet filled with blouses and skirts Mama sewed for her. She could crawl in the back and sit on the small shelf that held her jigsaw puzzles and books; it was dark and safe there. For her entire lifetime, she was glad this was the room where she had lost her virginity, you had to lose it somewhere, sometime, and this was the perfect place, her bedroom.

Married, she couldn't believe it. However, married or single, she was still pregnant, with an eleventh grade education. At a time when people counted days and months after weddings there would be no hiding the fact the baby was arriving much too early.

What will people say? They must have been saying plenty. Downstairs, Margaret stewed, worried and fussed. Her friends began asking questions and she just knew people were gossiping.

She nagged Lyle about the situation. All her plans for this girl, all the piano lessons, the money, the hopes, the dreams, college—everything gone, and upstairs a sixteen-year old pregnant daughter with a seventeen-year old husband. Without a job!

Maybe some of this might be her fault. Why did she let Bobby go to Cleveland and spend time with Harriet and Lucille? Why couldn't Lyle see what a terrible influence those awful women had on her child? Why?

We've spoiled her, given her too many things because she's been an only child for so long, before Linda was born. After all we've done for her and now this. Well, this is not what she wanted for her child's life; or her own.

Another visit to Dr. Johns with more tears and pleading from Margaret, and Dr. Johns finally relented, remembering the name of a doctor in Akron that would perform an abortion. Everything must be kept hush-hush, but it could be done. And while abortion doctors might be prosecuted if the authorities decided not to look the other way that would usually only happen if there were too many deaths of women frantically brought into local hospitals when the bleeding wouldn't stop. The women were rarely prosecuted, many of them dead or sterile from botched-up illegal abortions; they were considered victims.

Indeed, Margaret knew about a young woman on Red Brush Road, not a mile away, who had died last year from an illegal abortion. Although the woman was married, she already had three young children, two in diapers, the third going into first grade. She couldn't face having another child so soon and she found an abortionist. A dead mother with three kids, Margaret wondered what that poor, unfortunate woman's husband would do now with three little motherless kids. The neighbors gossiped. Talk. Talk. Talk…talk.

Dr. Johns assured Margaret this was a decent doctor with no criminal complaints.

Relieved at the prospect of not becoming a father, Jimmy never objected to the abortion as he handed over the hundred dollars to Margaret. It had taken him years to save that much money, but if that was what it took to get him out of the situation, he considered it a small price to pay. How dumb can you get, first getting your girlfriend pregnant, and then agreeing to marry her?

"Mrs. Milford, here's the hundred dollars. If this works, I'm leavin' and join'n the Navy. I don't know why I agreed to marry her anyway," he warned Margaret, when she had demanded the money for the abortion.

"Fine with me," responded a resolute Margaret, "and good riddance, young man, and don't come back around here again. Ever. You've certainly managed to ruin my daughter and all the plans we've had for her."

Margaret confided in Eleanor, her closest friend and confidant, the one who gave Margaret the recipe for the orange juice toddy. Margaret worked for Eleanor. They had gradually become very good friends as the two women spent work days discussing their customers, while they sewed in Eleanor's sewing shop. Talk. Talk. Talk…talk.

Bobby heard Mama repeating some of the stories from the sewing room to Daddy, but the one she remembered most was about a lady having an affair with the local preacher. She always suspected it was Eleanor herself, married to a meek man who never seemed to utter a word.

One word described Eleanor: gorgeous. Bobby thought her to be the most sophisticated and beautiful woman in the whole wide word. Her big round brown eyes, shaded by long lashes, were the exact color of her shiny brown hair, always carefully styled at the beauty shop. She dressed in the latest fashions. Her dresses, original designs produced from her sewing room, were bright floral prints, worn with perfectly matched spiky high-heeled shoes and handbags of vivid colors, echoing the hues of the dress fabrics.

She knew Eleanor gave Mama the recipe for that awful orange stuff and Bobby wondered if Eleanor ever drank that…or, horrors yet, if Mama ever had a dose of that terrible stuff!

After Margaret secured the money from Jimmy, she and Eleanor confronted Bobby and told her of the purpose for the trip to Akron.

"You have no choice, Bobby. That boy will never have a job, he doesn't love you and he's planning to leave for the Navy. He just told me. After all we've done for you; you're only being selfish if you refuse to have this operation." Margaret was determined, and Eleanor stood behind Margaret, backing up the decision.

"Your mother is only thinking about your welfare, Bobby. Do as she says," confirmed Eleanor, reaching up to put a stray hair in place, then fastidiously reaching down to pick a stray piece of lint from her dress.

A frightened and intimidated Bobby looked at the two women, and then thought about Jimmy not wanting her. Mama said he was leaving her. When she heard Eleanor, whom she admired and trusted, advise her to have the operation, she agreed to go with them.

Margaret became uneasy as they searched for the doctor's office. They drove into a neighborhood, a run down, littered, dirty area, located near the rubber tire company—the seediest place in town.

She hadn't expected it to be in the most respectable medical area near the hospital in Akron, but this?

Finally, they spotted a couple small numbers on the front of a smudged window of an empty littered office, which once was obviously a real estate business. Ninety Treemont Street. Yes, that was it, but no doctor sign. All they could see was an arrow pointing up a dirty flight of wooden stairs alongside of a doorbell. The only sign was the one scrawled on a box top, thumb tacked near the doorbell: "Ring for Service". As Margaret slowly lifted her finger up to push the doorbell, she realized she was trembling. The buzzer rang, instantly unlocking the door. Both she and Eleanor grabbed the crumbling wooden door and pulled it open, exposing the flight of dirt-encrusted gray stairs, dimly lit with only one bare bulb at the top of the landing.

Years later all Bobby could remember about that office was wooden-brown dingy, occupied by six mismatched wooden ladder-back chairs, one chipped lamp and three magazines.

Nothing about the place resembled the elaborate oncology and plastic surgery offices she would eventually visit.

As they sat in the waiting room, no one spoke a word until Eleanor leaned over, nudged Margaret and whispered, "Look, Margaret, under the chair…a microphone."

Only when it was obvious who Margaret, Eleanor and Bobby were, and why they were there from overheard small conversation, did a nurse enter the waiting room to usher them in to see the doctor. They waited thirty-three minutes in that brown, dingy room with six mismatched wooden ladder-back chairs, one chipped lamp, three magazines…and a hidden microphone.

Horrible, almost intolerable, pain for a sixteen-year old, as the doctor inserted something into her. The only anesthesia was something Mama called laughing gas.

It was after they returned home the labor pains began.

Would they never stop? They seemed to go on endlessly before Bobby felt the release of a tiny body. Too weak and afraid to pull herself up to look, she asked Mama what it was, she just had to know. Margaret grimly replied, "A boy. Now be quiet a little longer and don't look. Keep your eyes shut."

A frightened, exhausted Bobby tightly closed her eyes, obeying her mother. She couldn't see, however she could hear, and she heard the unmistakable rustle of newspaper and knew mama was wrapping her baby in the paper. Then she heard the old screen door slam and for some unexplained reason Bobby also knew what Mama was doing with her baby. Mama was taking her baby to the secluded burning drum in the field, back of the barn.

Beneath her she could feel moisture all the way up her back. She knew she hadn't urinated. Knowing it must be a blood, she became more terrified. When Margaret returned, she was still lying there with her eyes clenched tightly shut, as her mother instructed.

"Mama, I'm sure I've got blood all the way up my back. Mama, I'm scared, and I hurt all over," and Bobby started to cry.

Margaret was prepared, "Here, we'll get those sheets from under you and put clean ones on the bed. Here's a washrag. Wash off your back, and then slip into this fresh nightie. Put on this pad after you wash, you'll stop bleeding soon. You'll have to rest, stay off your feet for a few days and it'll all be over. You'll be okay. No one will ever know, and we'll never talk about this again. Forget this ever happened. It's over."

No one knew, but she did. It was country, it was 1947, and a youthful sixteen-year old just knew there was no God and if there were one she prayed he was too busy in heaven with other people to know the horrible sin she had just committed.

Neither Bobby nor Margaret ever talked about it, ever again, but neither did either one ever forget what happened that sunny summer day in 1947.

In the fall, it was time to go back to school and Bobby went, because of a chance meeting with her first-grade teacher, Mrs. Calhoun, one day. Mrs. Calhoun, the kind of a teacher every first grader would be fortunate to have, happened to be shopping in town. Like a gray-haired mother hen wearing glasses, she held those little ones in her ample lap, every class, every child, year after year. She never stopped caring, and never stopped thinking each child was her very own. When she saw Bobby, she talked to her like a mother.

"Go back to school Bobby, at least get your high school diploma. It'll only take a few months and you'll never be sorry," she kindly advised, in one of those defining moments that can change a life forever.

"Young lady, I don't want you here, but there's nothing legally I can do about it," Principal Walters warned a chastened Bobby, and that was just because she was married. Thank God, he didn't know about the doctor in Akron.

Along about mid-semester, Principal Walters caught up with her one day in the hall. Grabbing her by the arm, he made direct eye contact, informing her, "I owe you an apology," he said, "you've done a fine job here, under a difficult situation."

Bobby had really tried. She stayed to herself, kept her mouth shut, and hadn't divulged any "married talk" to morally contaminate the other students. She also managed to make the honor roll every semester, but she still felt like an outcast.

That year the senior play was "Snafu." She knew it stood for situation normal, all fouled up, but in later years Bobby always recited "Snafu", situation normal, all fucked up, to herself when things went wrong, and they very often did. It helped, sometimes.

In May, when she walked across the stage to collect her diploma, Principal Walters winked and congratulated her, "Job well done, Bobby, I'm proud of you," and shifting his eyes to the front row he continued, "and I know they are also."

Jimmy sat in the front row with Mama and Daddy.

In the front row, Margaret watched her daughter collect the diploma. It was okay, it all worked out okay, and her daughter would have a decent life without the stigmatism of pre-marriage pregnancy. There wouldn't be any infamous "shotgun wedding" for people to gossip about for her daughter, that anyone could prove anyway.

God forgive her, she had killed her first grandbaby. She hadn't thought the baby would be that big. She hadn't really considered about what would come after the doctor inserted the instrument. She thought it would just be a bloody mass, not a fully formed baby. She was just trying to protect her child, get rid of that problem like the summer when she discovered a batch of pinworms in Bobby, when she was a little girl.

Margaret briefly closed her eyes. Killing those pinworms was nothing like killing that baby boy. She couldn't forget the smell of the burning flesh as she stood by the burning drum that day. She had to add more gasoline and paper to get it all over with, and she shuddered at the memory. But it was done, she would forget about it. She couldn't change it, and her shoulders were broad, she just wouldn't think about it anymore.

There would be other grandbabies. She had just been a good mother, only doing her duty.

It wasn't too late for her daughter to be somebody, go to college and become a concert pianist, if only she would get rid of that lazy Jimmy. Margaret wondered why he hadn't left for the Navy, like he promised.

Bobby was wearing her first pair of high-heeled platform shoes and that night as she walked across the stage to collect her diploma she turned both heels completely under, ruining them. It didn't matter, she was floating on air. She had done something right—finally.

She thought about her baby boy, "Could she ever forget that sin? God was surely going to punish her for doing that."

An uninterested, discontented Jimmy watched Bobby walk across the stage and trip on those ridiculous high-heeled shoes. What a clumsy oaf. Wished he was home drinking a beer. It had been almost a year since he had been trapped into marrying this dumb girl and he didn't want a wife or any snot-nosed kids. The Navy rejected him, but he had new plans.

CHAPTER TWO

JIMMY NOTMAN

She was lying on her stomach reading when she felt the flutter. It was an odd sensation, like a little wiggly worm. No, it was too gentle; it reminded her of one of those little yellow field butterflies, gently fluttering its wings in the wind while it flits from one flower to another.

It had been a year since graduation. During that year Daddy and Grandpa Milton built Jimmy and Bobby a small square-shaped house in the vacant lot on the other side of Grandma and Grandpa's house. At Bobby's insistence, the square house was built with a dome center roof, high in the center with all four equal sides of the roof ascending up to the center dome. It looked like a large dollhouse in the middle of the field.

"Or a small church," Jimmy thought to himself, "all they had to do was put a friggin' cross on top of that damned house and they could pass the collection plate every Sunday morning. That's a good racket, maybe I'll get into that business someday when the time is right."

Jimmy sat on the sofa and watched Bobby getting ready to go to town with Margaret and thought what a mess he had made of his life. She was gaining more weight, the house was a mess, and so far his plans hadn't gone the way he wanted them. As she went out the door, he wondered how he ever thought this slob would make him happy, and to boot, she was a terrible cook. She was too dumb to get anything done right.

Margaret pinched her lips together as she sat in the car eyeing her daughter, "Well, you're not going anywhere with me looking like that. Go home and change your clothes, you look terrible. You look absolutely fat in that thing. And do something with your hair; it looks like a rat's nest today, when did you wash it last?"

Bobby sighed and slowly walked the short spaces between the three houses. Only one more dress would fit and she put it on. She looked in the mirror, ran a comb through her hair, told Jimmy goodbye again, and retraced her steps to Margaret, impatiently waiting in the car—ready to go to town.

As Bobby got in the car her mind flew back to that big white bathtub. Well, at least this time she wasn't naked.

"Okay, when are you planning on telling me? It's obvious you're pregnant again. Have you told Jimmy yet? That'll make his day, I'm sure. Never saw such a lazy boy, always running off playing baseball. Who do you think is going to support a baby? It won't be me and your dad, not after all we've already done for you." Margaret was thoroughly disgusted with her daughter.

In the next few months Bobby sat for hours, carefully hand-sewing small blue and white kimonos and matching bibs, gently folding each one, and tenderly placing them in a drawer in anticipation of the new baby boy.

Auntie Lucille came from Cleveland and stayed with her, patiently teaching her how to crotchet tiny blue booties; showing her how to stretch the yarn over the shiny needles.

Margaret fumed, "I suppose you're going to name that baby after your father's family, they are always around here now. Will it be Hattie, or maybe Lucy?" she sniffed.

"No, Mom. I'm sure it will be a boy and have decided to name him Dwight David," she had never considered it would be anything other than a boy. She wanted to bring her little baby to life again.

"Well, that's a stupid name, just a terrible name! You can't name a baby that. Where on earth did you ever hear of that name? At least have the decency to name it after the Myers' family, maybe it will grow up and become somebody. Not that lazy Jimmy will ever have the money to send it to college. You'll be lucky if he can even buy that baby diapers," Margaret claimed.

Bobby realized her mother was an expert at naming people. Grandma Milton had always been "Lyle's Mother"; Johnny was now "Lazy Johnny"; and she wouldn't repeat the names Mama had for Aunties Lucille and Harriet. Mama didn't even like her own youngest sister, Auntie Jane, only seven years older than Bobby. Margaret referred to Jane as "Pop's Bratty Favorite."

And Bobby was painfully aware Margaret referred to her as "Fat Bobby."

They could argue about the baby's name until hell froze over and it would never be called Dwight David. God must not have forgiven, he must have had a slow day in heaven two years ago and there would be no baby boy.

Jimmy and Bobby named the baby Cynthia Jo after his grandmother and Bobby always called her "Cindy Butterfly", because of those little yellow field butterflies that she first felt in her tummy.

After Cindy Butterfly was born, and Bobby realized God wasn't about to forgive her for that sin and send another little boy, she transferred the name of Dwight David to that little bit of life that burned up in a trashcan. He would forever be in her heart and prayers, and forever on her conscience. She was sure someday God was going to bellow down from the heavens and send a bolt of lightning at her and Jimmy for that sin. She made a pact with the Devil, she just knew it!

Meanwhile, Jimmy wasn't concerned about babies and names. He had other problems, problems Bobby knew nothing about. He sat in his car in a parking lot and stared sullenly at the factory entrance. That bitch. All he did was crook his finger at her. When she came over to him and asked what he wanted, the only thing he said was, "Oh, nothing, I just wanted to see if I could make you come with my finger."

Bonny, that dumb broad, had gone to the supervisor.

"Out, Notman, I won't have that kind of garbage around here. Collect your things and don't come back."

That old fart Johnson had no sense of humor and neither did Bonny. The bitch had been having sex with him in the back seat of the car for the last six months and now she had copped an attitude with him, just because he wasn't ready to leave yet.

When he saw Bonny come out of the factory door, he rolled down the window of his car and spoke to her, "Bonny, honey, comon'. Get in, let's talk about this. Ain't no cause to get so upset, it'll just take a little more time to get everythin' in order. Comon' honeypuss, we'll make it, you'll see."

Bonny Buttler pushed back her long blonde hair, glaring at him, "Won't work, not this time, Jimmy Notman. I saw her. She's pregnant again. Tell you what, when you're ready to take off for Nevada, call me. Until then, you can go straight to hell as far as I'm concerned."

Smiling, she climbed into her old Chevy. Now he had no job, one kid already, and a fat wife pregnant for the second time. If she knew Jimmy, it wouldn't take him long to decide to split. They could disappear in Nevada and wouldn't even have to worry about supporting that first kid and this new lump in Bobby's stomach.

Jimmy tore rubber getting out of the parking lot and on the way home he made his decision. He was tired of Bobby, what a dumb bitch. She was always pregnant. He and Bonny had sex every night after work for the past two months, what a lay, and she had never gotten pregnant. Maybe he was sterile anyway. Probably that kid wasn't even his and who knows who the latest one belonged to? It sure wasn't his. He had a plan, and it didn't include stupid, fat Bobby, whining, dirty snot-nosed kids or nosey in-laws, always breathing down his neck.

The old man was okay, but her old lady Margaret was just a big pain in the butt. Margaret had picked him up to go to the hospital the day Cindy had been born a few years ago and she actually said, "Well, you aren't going with me looking trashy like that. You need to shave, your shirt isn't even ironed, and just look at that hole in your pants." He had gone home and stayed. Drank a few bottles of beer, and by the time his stupid, fat wife called him about the baby, he didn't give a good Goddamn one way or another what the baby was, or what they were going to name the stupid thing.

And that dumb, superstitious Bobby, always moaning about that trashcan baby. God was going to get them and something else silly about having a pact with the Devil. It was just a bunch of religious nonsense. She was so full of crap, just like her mother. He would be glad to escape from this friggin' mess, once and for all.

That Bonny was one hell of a woman, what a team they would make! He had read about Bugsy Siegel opening a casino called the Flamingo in Vegas a couple years ago. After the mob killed him, dozens of casinos were built and they were begging for dealers. He was going out there to be a dealer. Big money—he and Bonny could make big money there, live the big life.

The things that bitch Bonny could do with her mouth, she had even taught him a few things in the back of that car. He would put her to work; she could get a waitress job and do a few tricks on the side. She'd probably pull in more cash with that mouth and body of hers than Jimmy could make dealing at the tables.

He stopped on his way home, changed the oil in the old car, checked the tires, and called Bonny, who had been expecting the call. It was done, they were leaving! "Vegas, here we come," yelled Bonny, as she danced around the room in her small apartment in Ravenna, Ohio.

"But Jimmy, what if they don't hire you out there? Are you sure the job is waiting for you? What are we going to do about this house, and what am I going to tell my parents?"

A confused Bobby was full of questions.

"Bobby, you can tell them anything you want, but this is too good of a job to pass up. I'll call you as soon as I arrive and send money for the kid..." Johnny walked through the door without saying goodbye, looked back, and took a long look at that house in the field. He felt relief for the first time since he got himself into this mess.

Let somebody else put a cross on top of that friggin' house, he had bigger things planned. Vegas and Bonny looked like the Promised Land and they were headed for it...he and Bonny with her long blonde hair and magic mouth.

It had been months and Margaret was stewing. Lazy Jimmy was still working in Vegas and sending such little money Bobby had been forced to get a job typing for a local accountant. She was as big as a house. Margaret no longer cared what this new baby would be named; all she cared about was how Bobby was going to feed these grandkids of hers.

A practical Margaret didn't want lazy Jimmy back; she just wanted him to continue sending money.

"Marge, Frank down at the plant told me they fired Jimmy and he didn't go to Las Vegas alone…that Bonny Buttler disappeared at the same time. Rumor has it they went there together," Lyle told her.

"The whole thing is Bobby's own fault," Margaret accused, "always getting fat and pregnant. After all we've done for that girl and she isn't going to amount to a thing. You know what? She's turned out to be just like your man-hungry sisters. Well, we've still got Linda; at least she isn't boy crazy. She'll go to college and be like my family, instead of yours."

Margaret immediately walked down to the house with the domed roof and told Bobby about lazy Jimmy and Bonny being in Vegas together. Satisfied she had done her duty, she left Bobby sitting in the living room, pregnant and alone.

Bobby had been vacuuming the house before Margaret arrived with the news and after her mother left her sitting there, she realized the vacuum was still running. She angrily yanked the vac cord from the wall so hard she snapped the plug off the cord. Stupid! Snafu! Snafu!

"Damn him, I wish he were dead. Damn him. Damn him. Damn. Damn. Damn. I want him dead and her along with him. I wish they were burning up and rotting in hell…both of them!"

It was early morning when Sheriff Brown pulled up the driveway to the square house with the domed roof on Brady Lake Road. He hated this kind of a call. Place looks like a church, he thought, all it needs is a cross on top. He knocked, and when he saw a very pregnant woman holding a young child answer the door, he dreaded delivering this message even more.

"Mrs. Notman?" he asked, then continued, "Our office had a call from Las Vegas about a James Notman. Is he your husband?"

He could tell by her eyes he had the right woman and the right house, and then he inquired if Mrs. Notman had ever heard of a Bonny Buttler, before he told her the news.

As she closed the door, it took a moment for the news to really sink in. Bobby knew in her heart she wished them dead from the very soul of her being that very moment, just about the time they had both been killed by a rain of bullets sprayed on the street in Vegas. Both dead! She knew it, she knew it. She had made a pact with the Devil when she killed that baby boy and God was surely going to spew his wrath on both she and Jimmy. The Devil had heard her when she wished Jimmy dead, and now he was dead, along with Bonny. She had been granted her wish.

She knew she should feel remorse, but all she felt was revenge and hate for those two people. There was still uncontrollable evil in her heart, spreading through her entire soul like a hungry cancer. She could feel it, she felt like she was being suffocated and strangled by filthy gray hands, squeezed tightly around her neck. She couldn't breathe.

Acutely aware she would forever be lost and forever destined to the same fate as Jimmy, she immediately dropped to her knees to pray and ask for God's forgiveness.

She discovered she couldn't. She attempted a prayer for the second time, then the third but no words would come into her mind to be spoken. Somewhere in her soul, prayer just evaporated. The words wouldn't come; it was like trying to write a sentence with the words all blanked out.

How could she ever get redemption and salvation if she couldn't pray for it?

CHAPTER THREE

SURVIVAL LESSONS

If Auntie Jane hadn't shown up at the door, she later realized she would never have made it through the ordeal of having the baby. Auntie Jane held her when she cried and when she was in pain. It was Auntie Jane that took her to the hospital, when the time came.

"Don't you worry, Baby. God will look after you and these little ones. In the meantime, I'll be here to take care of you," Auntie Jane reassured her, as she bundled Bobby up and headed the old car toward Robinson Memorial Hospital.

After Bobby recovered from having the baby, determination and anger quickly crept into her soul. It was overpowering, it overcame her, possessed her and became a rage that she felt only the Devil could understand.

She wouldn't make another mistake and trust any man or God himself with her fate, regardless of Auntie Jane's innocent belief that God would take care of her and her babies. Auntie Jane didn't know about Dwight David burning up in that trash can, or about the pact with the Devil.

Auntie Jane wasn't aware she lost her ability to pray, that God never permitted Bobby entry into His world. There would never be any help or forgiveness from heaven. Further, she was past caring about any advice or help from a heavenly spirit she couldn't feel or see. She could do everything herself, and somehow, just somehow, she would.

She hated Jimmy Notman and that slut Bonny. She was glad they were dead, and vowed someday to stand on the exact spot where they died, she fervently wished and imagined, in puddles of blood. Huge puddles. She could see them both lying there, writhing in the blood, and trying to grasp those last precious moments of life. The bloody scene sustained her anger and determination.

She had learned a valuable lesson, and would never rely on just one man again; there would always be more than one in case...just in case. Being practical, she knew she needed a husband to support her, and was determined to provide for herself and the kids somehow if it meant marrying someone, anyone, just to survive. She and the kids were going to make it.

Still doing office work to make ends meet, to put food in the kids' mouths and buy food, she quickly realized the only way out of poverty was to find a rich husband. Deciding to make herself attractive, she went on a diet and starved herself, until she was thin. She didn't have money, but she had determination and a nagging mother, ready and eager to give advice.

"You shouldn't wear stripes going around, they make you look fat," Margaret warned her, and she listened.

"Your hair is a mess. Get it cut and for heaven's sake do something about the color, you look just like your Aunt Harriet," Margaret ordered, and she listened.

Margaret looked at her daughter. Frankly, fat Bobby had turned into a thin, quite attractive red-headed young lady, wise to the ways of the world.

"Now I don't want you getting pregnant again, you can't have sex until you find someone else to marry you. Don't be dumb again." Margaret was full of advice. Bobby discarded that one; she would do with her body as she wished from now on.

"Well, don't come to your father and me if you get in trouble again. After all we have done for you, and look what's happened. Linda needs all our attention now. Just be careful."

Bobby met Ted Davenport at work. He looked like that Reeves guy, the one who played Superman in the movies. Ted was handsome, sure of himself, with a nasty quick temper, but oh, he could be so charming at times. She was also dating her "backup", an older man, John Belk, who was dull, boring and old enough to be her father. But he had money and a home, assets vitally important to the young widow.

Bobby was holding out for marriage and Ted, being young and impulsive was the first one to propose. As far as Bobby was concerned, he had two important things going for him—he had a job and a hot, young body with a hard little bobby. Although she wasn't an expert about the size of bobbies, she was sure, however, that Ted had the littlest one she would ever see, or had seen so far, anyway. It didn't matter, he had a job. She held out long enough that Ted wanted to use his little bobby more often than Bobby was willing to accept it. After all, she was a good girl; she just couldn't do "those kinds of things" without wearing a wedding ring. More important, she needed financial security. That fact she didn't share with young Ted.

He was a Catholic, insisting they go to church every Sunday and also encouraging Bobby to go to classes to become Catholic. It was then Bobby realized she was still unable to communicate in any way with God.

"Bless me Father, for I have sinned...," her mind went blank. It happened every time she tried to recite any of the prayers, and she would have to type out the prayers to read them to the priest. It was honestly embarrassing. She couldn't even remember the Lord's Prayer, and she couldn't bring herself to confess the sin of killing Dwight David. She knew in her heart and soul that, although the priest had blessed her, that mortal sin was still not forgiven because she hadn't been able to confess it. There was no way she would ever get redemption and forgiveness. She had been a fool for even thinking or hoping it would ever change, and she finally gave up, convinced she was still doomed to hell for the ultimate sin.

"It doesn't matter," she told herself, "I'll use my body and brains. I'll raise these two kids, one way or another, but I'll do it."

She and the handsome, hot-tempered Ted were finally married by a Justice of the Peace. God would have nothing to do with the marriage, and as it turned out, it would be a short-lived honeymoon. If God wasn't looking after Bobby and the kids, an overly-concerned Lyle Milford, Bobby's dad, was.

It was early afternoon and kid sister Linda had just finished playing a game of rummy with Grandma Milton. Before she could cross the grass to get to her house, she heard the loud voices.

"Dad and Bobby?" she questioned, "Not possible, that had never happened before; it had always been Bobby and Mom."

She had never seen two people disagree as much as those two. She just stayed out of the way as much as possible and kept her mouth shut. "But Dad and Bobby? No way," she thought, but sure enough, as she reached the bottom step of their house, she could distinctly hear it was Dad and Bobby.

She sat down on the outside stone step, reached up and pulled off one of Margaret's hollyhock flowers planted near the entrance and studied it while the voices got louder.

"After all we've done for you and now you go marry Ted Davenport. He's a Catholic!"

"Dad, I enjoy going to that Catholic Church. Since when is anybody in this family concerned about God or religion?"

"Young lady, in case you have forgotten, this family sprouted from generations of New England Baptist Ministers," and Lyle lowered his voice again, realizing he had never shouted at either one of his girls before, "there's nothing wrong with being Catholic, but this family is Baptist, and don't forget it. I would be willing to bet Ted's family isn't so happy either about this marriage outside of their church."

Then he thought about his grandchildren and raised his voice again, "...and what about your two kids, you know he'll never be a decent father to them, he's got a terribly bad temper. And will he insist you raise your children Catholic? What about your family? You're selfish. Get rid of him, Bobby. Get rid of him. After all we've done for you..."

That last sentence really did it, she had been hearing that thrown at her for years by Margaret, but never Dad, and he had said it twice in the last five minutes. "What? What have you done for me?" Bobby vehemently loudly demanded.

"Oh, oh, Bobby's goin' to be soreeee," Linda said to herself.

She quickly shoved over to the side of the step as Lyle came storming out of the house, heading to the barn. Linda could see he was angry, very angry. His face was flushed and he looked like he may cry at any moment. As he headed for the barn, Linda rushed into the house to find Bobby.

She looked around for her mother, but Margaret was conveniently nowhere in sight, she wasn't home work yet, conveniently absent after she goaded Lyle into having a talk with Bobby.

Linda knew instinctively Bobby must have disappeared into her old bedroom, the one Linda moved into after Grandpa Milton and Dad built the house in the field for Bobby and Jimmy.

"Wow, I hope she doesn't want to move back again, that bedroom belongs to me now, and I won't give it back. Not me! If she thinks she's going to move back in here every time she loses a husband, she's nuts, no matter what Dad says," Linda muttered to herself. She loved her big sister dearly, but no way was she moving into that stinkin' back bedroom again.

Linda made the steps up to the second floor two at a time, hit the landing and turned left into the big bedroom that was hers now—straight to the bookcase. She pulled open the book she had carefully cut a little rectangle in to hide a pack of cigarettes, extracted a cigarette, lit up, and took a puff.

Bobby stopped crying, "Damn it, Linda, you're only twelve years old. What are you goin' to do if Mom and Dad find out you're smoking?"

Linda shrugged, "What the hell are they goin' to do 'bout it?"

Bobby, remembering how she shouted at Dad, started crying again, "I'm sorry," she said, mostly to herself.

"You should be," offered Linda, "Mom, yes, but Dad…how could you, after all he has done for us? You know…"

"Shut up! Bobby interrupted, "when I want your opinion I'll ask for it, and I'm not asking."

"You don't have to, I'm giv'n it to you anyway," and twelve-year old Linda walked over and gave her older sister the biggest hug she had ever been given. Linda figured it was a bigger hug than either Jimmy or

Ted had ever given her sister. She adored her big sister, but no way was she ever going to moon over men like Bobby did. Boys…gag, gag. Yuk! Yuk!

Later that evening Bobby returned to the apartment she and Ted rented in Ravenna when Ted refused to live so close to Margaret. He considered her a meddling troublemaker. They had been married only four months, twenty-five days and six hours. She knew better than to wish him dead, she just wished him gone.

And he was. She may not be able to communicate with God, but her old friend the Devil could still hear her.

It wasn't Sheriff Brown that delivered the predictable news this time, it was Deputy Lucie Fuehr.

The previous night a very angry, intoxicated Ted Davenport reacted to Bobby's announcement of a divorce by speeding away from the apartment. He wrapped his convertible around a telephone pole, instantly separating his young muscular body, with the hard little bobby, from his handsome head. His head was thrown in a ditch fifteen feet away.

CHAPTER FOUR

THE BACK-UP MAN

Bobby picked up the phone and called the backup, John Belk. Good, safe, boring John had been heartbroken when she told him she was marrying Ted a few months before.

"John? Honey, this is Bobby. Could you please come down here to see me? Things have happened, and I really need you quite badly. I have to talk to someone and you're the only one who truly understands me."

Bobby hung up the phone. That had been easy, it only took one "please."

Good old John, he would do in a pinch, and Bobby could hear one of Margaret's favorite expressions, "If you don't pinch too hard."

John Belk lived in Pineville, Ohio, about an hour's drive east of the Ravenna apartment and in exactly fifty-five minutes he was holding a tearful Bobby in his arms. He gritted his teeth as he listened to the story about Ted's frightful temper tantrums, how he became a monster when he drank, and how he hit poor Bobby. And he was mean to the little kids too—so unforgivable, a terrible way to treat precious Bobby and those two little darling babies.

As he consoled her, he realized this young woman really needed him to take care of her. He let her slip away once, it wouldn't happen a second time. Poor, dear, sweet delicate Bobby, with those two little fatherless children, she shouldn't have to work so hard, always worrying about feeding them. They needed someone to take care of them.

Bobby politely sniffled and caught a little sob in her sweet throat as she permitted John Belk to wipe away her tears with his clean handkerchief. She looked up at John and sighed as she settled into his huge arms. "He can pinch as hard as he wants," Bobby thought, "as long as me and the kids are in his will. I don't care what size his bobby is, but I sure hope it's going to be bigger than Ted's." Then she thought about his age, about fifteen years older than her own father…"And I hope it still works too." Oh, well, she'd tried two young husbands, it was time get practical, she had two kids to buy shoes for.

John Belk tenderly wiped away Bobby's tears, then gently kissed that sweet mouth, did he dare ask for more?

Bobby took his big hand and placed it over her heart, "Do you feel my heart beating, dear John? I just know it's beating so fast from your kiss."

John eagerly placed his hand over her heart and could feel the warm pounding, and then he slowly slid his hand and cupped it over her soft breast.

Bobby allowed a good feel before she lowered her eyelids and confessed, "Dear John, I have only known two men in my lifetime, the two men I was married to, and I could never just sleep around. I just couldn't do that, and you're too good of a God-fearing man to ask me to lower my standards."

"Could we be married?" she shyly asked.

John Belk looked at this helpless waif of a girl with the red hair and hazel-green eyes. Poor little widow, young enough to be his daughter, but as he felt himself harden he knew the feelings he was having in his pants had nothing to do with age or fatherhood. He wanted this woman in bed, and if marriage was the only way, he was up, literally speaking, to the task at hand.

"Bobby dear, little baby, we'll be married whenever you want and where you want. Just name it, anything is yours," John Belk promised.

Bobby placed her own small white delicate hand over John's hand as that big sturdy hand remained cupped over her breast, and from under her lashes she could see the obvious bulge in his pants getting firmer…and larger. She looked up at John from under her lashes and innocently asked, "Oh, John, how sweet, I do love you so. Could we be married in Las Vegas next week?"

CHAPTER FIVE

VEGAS HONEYMOON

John and Bobby spent the next week combining homes and families. A widower for many years, he had a son, Bart, a couple years older than Cindy Butterfly. They transported Bobby's furniture and clothes to John's big house next to the cemetery on the hill east of Pineville on Casement Avenue. That week they also attempted to blend the three kids into a harmonious family unit.

"This may be a bit difficult. They don't seem to like each other," she confided to Aunt Jane, when she arrived to watch the kids.

"Now don't you worry, Baby, you just keep your trust in the Lord and He'll take care of you and those little ones," assured Aunt Jane.

With Auntie left safely watching over the kids, John and Bobby drove to the airport where John lovingly slipped a huge diamond ring on Bobby's left hand. Immediately after arriving at McCarren Airport in Las Vegas, he whisked her away in a cab to a wedding chapel on the Vegas strip, where they were married.

John respected Bobby's wishes about premarital sex and during the previous week when they were combining homes and families they had slept in separate bedrooms. He waited to explore the rest of her inviting curvaceous body until after they were married, although a few times he must admit, his hands did stray to forbidden territory.

He stood in line to check into the hotel on Fremont Street in downtown Vegas and looked at his new bride and couldn't believe she was all his, forever. "What a beautiful, innocent young woman she is," he thought.

As Bobby stood with their luggage at her feet in the lobby watching John register, she thought, "Maybe he'll do. At least I've hooked a guy with money this time…he'll always be there to take care of us. We'll take care of the financial part first thing when we get back to Pineville. I'm sure not washin' any socks for nothing."

After they checked into the hotel and entered their room she embraced John, "Just give me a few minutes to freshen up, dear," and John understood. He eagerly removed the bedspread, turned down the covers of the bed, got undressed and layed down to wait. Remembering Bobby's soft breasts last week, he was more than ready for his bride.

He caught his breath when he saw Bobby come out of the bathroom dressed in a sheer black negligee. She was absolutely luminous, his bride, with her red hair brushed out, and her skin looked like cream. As she slipped into bed beside him, he was almost afraid to touch her. Then surprisingly, she came quickly into his eager arms.

She took his big hand and placed it over her bare breast under the sheer black nightie, "Oh, my Dear John, please leave on the lights. I want to see you; I've waited so long for you. You'll just never know how I've wanted you to make love to me, from that very first moment when you kissed me and put your hand over my breast last week. Just touch me, everywhere, and hold me. Make me forget all those bad things in the past. You know I'll love you and be your faithful wife for the rest of our lives. I've been so lonely."

John Belk swelled with pride. In fact, he swelled all over as he cupped her soft full breast, tenderly lifted the hem of the flimsy nightie and lowered his big hand between her smooth legs before he put his finger into her inner-most warm spot. It was moist. His wife, his darling precious little innocent wife really was ready for him, wanted only him. As he entered her, he could hear her give a little moan and cry, "Oh, John, my dearest, I do love you so."

The next morning Bobby crept quietly out of bed and quickly dressed. She glanced at her new husband, making absolutely certain he was safely asleep, before she craftily slipped out of the door. Taking the elevator to the lobby, she left the hotel. She had a motive when she asked John Belk to take her to Las Vegas, and it wasn't to see one of those mushroom atomic clouds they were shooting off here, or to enjoy any honeymoon with an old man.

She hailed a cab that quickly transported her to the corner between the Flamingo and Barbary Coast Casinos on Las Vegas Boulevard where she knew that rain of bullets had mowed down Jimmy and Bonny a few years before. She had waited a long time and had something to say to both of them. She passionately knew their souls remained there on that bloody spot, "Jimmy, see, I told you we had a pact with the Devil, we killed Dwight David, you, me, and Margaret. He burned up in a trashcan, and we'll pay for that sin."

Standing there on the corner, the knowledge she had a destiny with death in Vegas, along with Jimmy, became more than a possibility, she knew it was reality; and someday her fate would surely end up here in this neon city. She could feel it, and the idea both fascinated and repelled her, compelling her to continue, "You bastard Jimmy, I wished you both dead and I don't regret one minute of it. Until my Vegas destiny comes and we both pay for our terrible sins, I'm going to enjoy every minute of my life. Furthermore, I hope you and that trashy blonde bitch are rotting in hell."

John stirred in bed when Bobby entered the room, carrying hot coffee and doughnuts. "Bobby, sweetheart, where have you been? I woke up about five minutes ago and wondered where you were."

"Oh my dear heart, I'm sorry I made you worry; I just went down to the coffee shop to get your breakfast. Let's just stay in here all day and be together. Oh, John, make love to me again, sweetie. I've been so lonely and I've needed you so badly."

She slowly and deliberately removed all of her clothes in front of John, lying in the bed waiting. With the drapes drawn and the lights on, she slid out of her filmy dress, hung it up, bent over, unhooked both garters, and slowly rolled down each sheer nylon stocking. She reached around to her back, deftly unsnapped her bra, permitting her breasts to fall free. She then slid down her black lace panties, standing totally nude above her new husband lying on the bed.

She demurely crossed her arms over her breasts making sure most of them showed to their fullest advantage above her little triangle of reddish pubic hair as she stood over him.

John was responding just watching her, he could feel himself getting hard. How modest she was, his bride, trying to cover those lovely breasts with her precious little fragile hands.

She lowered herself to the bed, softly pleading, "Oh John, make love to me all over. Kiss me everywhere, no one has ever done that to me, and I want you to be the first one. Oh, my dearest John, teach me how to do everything. I've been so lonely."

He couldn't wait any longer and he entered her quickly, and then held back. Realizing what she was requesting, he withdrew and lowered his head and slowly began to kiss her, commencing at those sweet-smelling toes and working his way upward. As he ran his tongue through that sweet little triangle of curly hair he could feel himself almost exploding. His little young innocent bride, he would make love to her as no one else ever had before.

"Not bad…," Bobby mused to herself, "for an old man. He's older than Dad, but just maybe life's goin' to be interestin' after all, but we'll hav'ta take care of that Will thingie soon as we get back to Ohio. Be damned if I'll wash a man's socks without bein' in his Last Will and Testament. A girl has to be practical…," and as she felt him enter her once more, she thought, "…thank goodness, at least it's bigger than Ted's, and this guy seems to know what to do with it too!"

"Oh, John, oh my Dear John, it feels so good. My darling, please don't ever stop," she softly commanded.

And he didn't.

CHAPTER SIX
LAST WILL AND TESTAMENT

Bobby felt a rush of honest affection as she watched John slowly sign most of his assets over to her. Although, she thought, it's about time—five and a half years. "Patience," she told herself, over and over again.

John made provisions for Bart's college education, but the bulk of his estate would go to her and their new baby when it arrived. She would have the big house on Casement Street, the cars, and most of his retirement. Dear, sweet John, she thought, and all it took was getting her very pregnant. Regardless of the reason, she would never have to worry ever again how to keep food on the table or shoes on the kids' feet.

She would never have to work outside of her home again, if she didn't choose to do so. It would be her decision. John brought her freedom and security…finally.

Margaret sniffed and rolled her eyes five years ago when they were married.

"What on earth do you want with an old man like that? Why, he's a good fifteen years older then your father. Are you crazy? For heaven's sake, Bobby, what good will he ever be for you?"

Lyle had searched Bobby's eyes and asked, "Is he good to you and the kids?"

"Yep, Dad, he's the best."

"That's all that's important, honey. Bring him around and maybe he'll be a good fishing buddy 'round here."

Attorney Sid Chapman watched both of the Belk's sign the reciprocal Last Will and Testaments his secretary had just finished typing. Sid's two secretaries witnessed the signings and Sid explained to the Belk's he would keep the original wills in his safety deposit box at the bank, two floors down.

As he handed the copies of the wills to John, he couldn't help but observe what an attractive couple. Obviously a May-December union, John Belk must be at least sixty, probably old enough to be her father. Yet somehow they looked like they belonged together. "What a petite delicate woman she is," he thought, "in spite of the fact that she's very pregnant. John must not be too old to keep that little fireball happy. Good God, by the time that baby will hit kindergarten I would lay odds I'll be filing that Last Will and Testament in Probate Court for Mrs. Belk. And by all indications she'll never have to worry about finances when the time came. Smart woman, I bet there's an interesting story about this woman. Certainly it was a marriage of convenience on her part."

Sid stood up and watched John help Bobby up from her chair and gently place her coat over her shoulders, and then he opened the door of Sid's office for her. A queen, that's how John Belk treated his wife, a red-headed, green-eyed queenie.

He was still thinking about her as he closed his office door behind the Belk's and sat back down in his comfortable chair. A queenie, a red-headed, green-eyed queenie, would that make John a king? It had been a long day and the idea amused Sid Chapman. He rocked back in his big brown leather chair and let loose one of his infamous bellowing laughs. It started as a rumble in his midriff, traveling up through his throat and by the time it reached his mouth it erupted into a jumble of cackles. At that exact moment, because Sid was such a tall, big man, his right leg automatically popped up and thumped against the inner part of his desk.

Yep, Sid wouldn't mind being a king for that red-headed queenie, pregnant or not!

There he goes again, observed Melanie sitting outside his closed door in the reception room. She heard the cackle of laughter, waited for the thump on the desk and turned to Patty, the other office girl, "What do ya' s'pose that's all about, he usually only laughs and thumps like that when he's talk'n to his girlfriends."

After John and Bobby left Sid's office, John helped Bobby into the car. "Poor little darling," thought John, "and such a good mother. Makes most of the kids' clothes, even sews the boys' shirts and gives 'em haircuts. She's such a good, loving wife and never asks for much for herself."

She had only asked him for two things since they married: a concert grand piano and a yearly trip back to Las Vegas to celebrate their anniversaries. John saw that she got both things, and he would have tried to give her the moon, if she had asked for it.

Every year he took her back to Vegas and sweet Bobby would leave their room, bringing his breakfast to him like she did that very first morning of their honeymoon. Five years—and she still came back and undressed for him, slipped into bed and they would make love.

It was the fifth year he had gotten her pregnant. He mused, "Not bad for an old man, John Belk. Now it will be yours, mine and ours."

When Melanie went home that night she related the story of the Belk appointment, followed by Sid's laughing and thumping, to her husband, "It sure is interesting; working in that office," she declared.

"Yeah," grumbled her husband, "and if ever lays one hand on you, or even buys you one present, you're outta' there, honey."

"Don't be silly, Bob, he has a whole stable of Pineville women at his beck and call. Don't know why his wife doesn't catch him."

CHAPTER SEVEN
YOURS, MINE AND OURS

Fighting, Arguing. The next little old lady that stops and tells me these are the best years of my life I'm going to belt her. Or barf. As if she hadn't barfed enough with this pregnancy. Pragmatic, scheming Bobby was beginning to doubt her sanity by the time the new baby arrived.

John Belk looked radiant. A new father and almost sixty years old! He packed Bobby's suitcase and bundled her up to take her to the hospital for the baby's arrival, and he arranged for Auntie Jane to take care of the other three kids. He also named the new baby, taking the names from his own initials—Jeffery Blaine Belk.

Within six or seven months Bobby wondered how she was ever going to survive, as much as she loved these kids they were absolutely driving her crazy!

"I want the window!" demanded Cindy.

"No, it's my turn," argued Bart.

"No, Mom, he had it last time!" Cindy yells.

"I did not!"

"Yes you did…tell him Mama, I did too!"

"Well, you can't have this side," countered Randy as he squeezed past both of them and grabbed the coveted seat. The little bugger sat there smiling like a checkered tabby cat lapping up a bowl of milk, with his little arms folded, daring either Cindy or Bart to try to get to the window.

"Mamaaaaaaaaa…make Randy move!"

Snafu! Snafu!

Bobby quickly scooped up baby Jeff and put him in the middle of the front seat of the car between John and her, "Okay kids, just wait a minute, until I get out the tape," with that, Bobby pulled a roll of Scotch tape out of the glove compartment and methodically pulled off four three-inch sections of the tape and pasted them on the dashboard of the Impala. She'd never actually tape any mouths shut to stop the arguments and noise, but the kids didn't seem to know that.

Little kids, little problems. The problems became bigger as the kids aged. A few years later a disgruntled, teen-aged Cindy Butterfly pouted and cried that Bobby and John absolutely ruined her birthday party and social life when they insisted all the lights remain on in the den instead of turned off.

"My first boy-girl party and you've ruined it; we weren't doin' anything with the lights off, Mom. Honest!" as she tried to convince a suspicious Bobby, "All the other kids do it."

"Well, I don't care about all the other kids, I only care about you, and the lights remain on at this party."

And she and John wondered if they'd ever survive the teenaged motorcycle years with the boys.

Jeff was running to tell Randy, "Randy, she is really goin' to do it, ya' better give her the keys."

"Naw, she'll never do it, she's just threatnin'…I ain't gonna give her no keys," drawled Randy, with big brother bravado.

"Yes she is Randy, yes she is. She has your baseball bat, and she says she's gonna beat your cycle…please Randy, she is really goin' ta' do it. All ya' have to do is give her the keys like she asked ya' tooooo…," then they heard the obvious sound of wood hitting metal coming from Randy's bedroom.

That evening Jeff laughed at Randy, "Randy, I don't think it was because you disobeyed her when you took that cycle downtown, and then wouldn't give her the keys. It was because you took it over her new carpet."

"Those kids are lucky I used it on the cycle instead of them," Bobby groused later to John, "Bet they'll never take that dirty thing over my carpet again."

"I'll never survive," thought Bobby as she typed up her resume and went on job interviews to find a job, "As much as I love these kids, I've got to get out of this house to save my sanity. They can't grow up too quickly for me; if these are the best days of my life, then my life is the real pits."

Maybe Margaret was right after all, why had she married this old man and had this houseful of kids?

Then she thought about John's Last Will and Testament…and the thought momentarily crept into her mind…maybe she would just wish another husband dead.

CHAPTER EIGHT
VEGAS ANNIVERSARY

Seventeen years and John wondered where the years had gone. They had been happy years for him. After he married Bobby, his home on Casement Street had turned into a noisy, joyous family home, and now the kids were almost raised, and John was enjoying his retirement years.

John's fishing buddy, Lyle, had also retired and he and Margaret moved to Florida, along with Linda, who was now a high school teacher. John thought about how he looked forward to great Florida fishing trips with Lyle next year.

Bobby could keep Margaret occupied. That was certainly one critical old lady, probably in the first stages of what the entire family referred to as "The Myers' Curse" like her father B.T. before her. B.T., now in his nineties was in a nursing home in Alliance, Ohio in the advanced stage of the family curse.

Both the older kids had married in that huge white house with the wrap-around rocking chair porch on Casement Street. They were big, joyous, family weddings. First, Bart married Rita, a local Pineville girl and then a few years ago Cindy Butterfly married Richard, the boy from across the street that was once their paperboy. Cindy quickly made John and Bobby grandparents, two little blonde girls named Lori and Jennifer. Randy and Jeff, the two younger boys, were still going to school: Randy at River High and Jeff at Jefferson Township Elementary, both near their Casement Street home.

True to his word, John flew Bobby to Vegas to celebrate their anniversary, and as usual they were checked into the Flamingo Casino. "What a wonderful woman," he thought, "my wife, just as tiny and petite in middle age as she was when I made her my bride, right here in Vegas seventeen years ago today."

He heard Bobby bringing in his breakfast and watched her undress for him, a routine he still enjoyed after all these years and he still became aroused as if it were their wedding day. "Well, almost," he mused.

As he watched her reach around to unhook her bra, he remembered how he had made love to her on their honeymoon. At that exact moment he felt the tightening in his chest, it came into him like a bolt of lightening. He gasped and fell over in the bed.

She unhooked her bra, and reached down to remove her panty hose when she glanced at John. She still loved to watch John's eyes on her as she undressed. Then she saw his eyes widen as he grabbed his chest, heard the unmistakable gasp, and saw his eyes roll back into his head.

She grabbed the phone in a panic, "This is room 666, send paramedics at once or an ambulance. Quick!" she screamed into the phone, "I think my husband has just had a heart attack or a stroke. Oh, please send someone quickly," she pleaded to the operator.

Bobby threw on a robe and ran out into the hall, and within minutes the paramedics were there. She hastily directed them into room 666, where John was sprawled out wide-eyed on the bed, stiffly grasping his chest with one of his hands. She was helpless, all she could do was watch in horror as the three men and one woman worked over John, vainly trying to revive him.

The hotel manager, Mr. Leslie, arrived and took Bobby into a lounge to gently explain there was nothing else that could be done. He would make all the arrangements for a local funeral home to transport the casket to the airport. They were just waiting for the coroner. Bobby sat dazed, with tears dripping down her cheeks, signing the necessary forms Mr. Leslie had given to her. Dear John, dear, Dear John, he had been so good to her and the kids, and she had depended on him for so many years.

Conveniently forgetting last week's fleeting wishes about collecting on his Last Will and Testament, she rationalized maybe she hadn't been madly in love with him, but she respected him and had been a good, faithful wife and friend to him during their marriage. It was all a huge mistake, John couldn't be dead, and how could she go on without him? "Why? Why? Why John?" she asked herself.

"Madam, I'll call the airline. Do you have someone to meet you at the airport in Ohio?" Mr. Leslie inquired.

"Yes, you can call my daughter, Cindy Steiner. Here's her number, I'm sure she will meet me; please tell her I'll call her later tonight. And thank you for all your help, Mr. Leslie. I'll be fine now, honestly." Bobby reassured him as she handed him a piece of paper with Cindy Butterfly's home phone number written on it.

"Mrs. Belk, I've had the bellhop gather up your things, we have taken the liberty of repacking them and putting them in another room for you tonight where you'll be more comfortable. If there is anything else we can do for you, please just lift up the phone and call my office directly," Mr. Leslie told her.

He was concerned about Bobby because she quickly transformed from a grief-stricken frenzied woman into a calm, almost serene lady. Totally calm and in control, as if she were waiting for him to leave, so she could run an errand.

Gus DeHavilland had been the doorman at the Flamingo Casino almost since the doors first opened in the 40's and he had seen a lot of people come and go during those years.

He was the first black doorman on the strip, but he never told anyone about his heritage. No one hired blacks in the Vegas casinos. He was a light-skinned offspring of a mulatto woman and an Irish man, making Gus a quadroon. His birth certificate still said he was black, and he left New Orleans at a young age to find anonymity and a job on the Las Vegas strip. Passing as white was easy, because Gus looked more like a dark Latino than the one-fourth Negro origin he knew he was. He passed out of necessity, not because he was ashamed of his ancestors.

Gus DeHavilland was a proud, honest man who enjoyed observing the people coming through the door of the Flamingo. His job was his life and was very good at it. Standing by the door, he loved watching the world pass by and year after year he would often observe the same people coming and going.

"Well," he thought, "there she is again...the little redhead is back." He noticed her that first year, over fifteen years ago; because she stood on the exact place those two young people had been shot way back in the early 50's. That had sure been one bloody day. At first he didn't understand what she was doing standing there, with her lips moving. Gus was certain she wasn't praying. Then one time he managed to walk close enough to her and heard her say the word "snafu."

Gus had been around enough army bases and soldiers to know what that meant for sure. This was one angry lady and she was there in that same spot every year. He could set a clock by her yearly appearance.

"Michael, I'll bet you twenty bucks that red-headed woman shows up this morning at seven o'clock. She'll stand right outside on the sidewalk and look like she is praying; only her face will be angry."

Young Michael, working the concierge desk, thought it was a sure bet. He whipped out a twenty dollar bill, only to be confronted by the exact scene described by Gus at the exact time, seven o'clock.

"Gus, you old con-man, how did you know?"

"Happens every year, Michael. Here's your twenty bucks back and let that be a lesson to you about gambling on a sure thing with an old man," Gus affectionately advised, as he returned the money, placing a friendly hand on Michael's shoulder.

After that young Michael never again bet with Gus about this red-headed lady, but every year the two casino workers would pass a knowing smile between them when she arrived. She never failed to appear.

But what was she doing here at this time of day? She had been there her normal time that morning, but it was 5:30 in the afternoon, almost time for his shift change. Gus sensed something was wrong, and he stayed to keep an eye on her. In recent years, she reminded him of a widow going to her husband's grave to talk to the departed...an angry widow.

Bobby slowly walked to the spot where she stood every year talking and cursing Jimmy and reminding him about their sins and pact with the Devil because of killing Dwight David. Only it wasn't Jimmy Notman and Bonny that she was cursing now.

"God, I know you can't hear me. I don't even believe you are out there somewhere. You're just a Santa Claus to keep adults from sinning. Do you hear me? Do you hear me, you great big Santa Claus in the sky? When we are little kids we believe in Santa Claus and if we are bad, he brings us a lump of coal. When we get to be big kids we call you God, and if we are sinners you bring us the fires of hell and total damnation. Can you hear me, you big fake up there?" She was shouting.

She raised her clenched fist upward. "Vegas is my destiny, not John's. Me and Jimmy, we're the sinners. You got the wrong person in that room. You took the wrong person," and she shook her fist to heaven, located somewhere over that bright Vegas umbrella sky.

There was no answer. There was no bolt of lightning from the transparent blue Vegas sky. Overhead, there just a calm Nevada sky temporarily interrupted by a plane on its final approach into McCarran Airport a couple miles away. On the strip in front of her was an endless parade of cars and buses honking their horns and blowing out exhaust fumes, totally oblivious to her outburst and raised fist. No one had noticed, and God still ignored her. Total silence from the heavens and she was not about to be ignored any longer!

She loudly, angrily persisted, "Damn you, God, damn you, damn you, damn you...you can't hear my prayers, but maybe you can hear my curses," and with that blasphemous outburst she collapsed to the ground, on the exact spot where Jimmy Notman had bled to death years before.

Although the cars and pedestrians were oblivious to the raging woman shouting at the sky, punctilious Gus DeHavilland, however, was scrupulously watching her, and when he saw her raise her fist then collapse, he quickly summoned the front desk and Mr. Leslie. He ran out onto the sidewalk and cradled her in his arms until Mr. Leslie arrived, about five minutes later.

By that time Bobby revived a bit, enough for Gus and Mr. Leslie to help her back into her room and make sure she was comfortable for the night.

"Madam, we'll have the casino limo pick you up and take you to the airport tomorrow morning. Are you sure your daughter will be waiting at the Akron airport for you?" inquired a concerned Mr. Leslie.

He then turned to Gus and instructed, "Gus, bring a cold cloth for Mrs. Belk's forehead."

Gus quickly complied with Mr. Leslie's order and as he gently laid the washrag across Bobby's forehead, he felt compelled to say, "Mrs. Belk, I look forward to see'n you next year. Will you still be com'n to see us, we'd like to see you again, Ma'am, anytime." He had come to know this lady; he finally knew her name and felt a responsibility for her.

"Yes Gus, I still have a good reason to visit Vegas," replied Bobby, now quite sure she was preordained to a fateful destiny here in this city. It was a fate she wished upon Jimmy and a fate that now claimed John. It was just a matter of time, and she was more positive than ever she someday had a destiny with death in Las Vegas, because of her sins and the repulsive pact with the Devil himself.

She would be back.

CHAPTER NINE
CONDOLENCES

    Ohio skies were overcast, doomsday gray, as the pilot lined up for the final approach into the Akron airport. The tower cleared him for landing and he lowered the landing gear, then the flaps. He lined up with the runway, waited until the plane glided to within a few feet of the concrete, adeptly pulled up on the nose, and let the plane settle down naturally until he felt the wheels make squealing contact with the smooth runway. Then he expertly taxied the plane into the empty airport gate and congratulated himself on another perfect three point landing.
    "Ladies and Gentlemen, use care when opening those upper baggage compartments. Shift happens, you know," he joked over the intercom, attempting to amuse passengers, weary from the long flight from Vegas.
    They were all waiting for her, Bart and Rita, Cindy Butterfly, Jeff and Randy. Cindy's Richard was nowhere in sight, and Bobby briefly wondered where he was and why wasn't he here with the rest of them. She also wondered just what the hell do you tell your kids at a time like this? Nothing, they didn't need words, they just needed one another. They all met her and there were hugs and kisses all around. Bart, John's oldest son, had thankfully taken care of the funeral arrangements in Ohio, and Bobby was so thankful for this precious young man, her stepson, whom she had grown to love as much as her own flesh and blood.

Looking at her children, she again thought of how wonderful John had been to them all. They had grown into wonderful young adults, a yours, mine and ours family that had, by some unexplained miracle, blended into one family, sharing their good times and bad. There was just no way would anyone have guessed they all hadn't emerged from the same genetic pool.

They buried John in McConnellsville, a southern Ohio town where he had grown up, and still had relatives living there. As Bobby sat in the car, she surveyed the town square and the local restaurant called simply, The Dinner Bell. What a happy childhood her husband must have had here in this pleasant little village. They had all been happy in Pineville, but she couldn't help thinking what a perfect place this would have been to raise a family. They should have come here years ago.

Once they returned home to Pineville it all seemed like an unpleasant nightmare and life became stark reality again. There were thank-you letters to write in return for all the flowers and letter of condolences she and the kids received. John and she accumulated many friends over the years and she heard from most of them before or after the funeral.

Margaret called from Florida, "Well, it's too bad, but what did you expect when you married a man that old? You must have known this would happen. Well, just dry your tears and quit feeling sorry for yourself, it isn't the end of the world, you know. It happens to everyone sooner or lat…"

Lyle interrupted, he had heard enough, "Marge, hand me the phone."

"Bobby? Are you and the kids okay? We'll drive up to Ohio if you need us, do you have enough money?"

"Dad, we're fine, really, it will just take time, it's a big adjustment for the kids, Bart and Jeff are especially affected. It all came so unexpectedly. Just tell Mom I love her and I'll talk to her later…I love you too, Dad."

It seemed as if the telephone calls were endless. "Mother, Ben Morrison is calling for you," Cindy Butterfly announced as she handed the phone to Bobby.

"Hello Ben. Thank you for calling. Yes, we'll truly miss him and I know you will also, you've been such a good friend to us both for so many years. Please extend my thanks to all of the workers at the plant for the flowers…yes, of course, you can call me anytime, you always have, you know."

Ben, who had been John's immediate supervisor before his retirement, had always been helpful and from the moment they had met there had been an attraction. A woman can feel those things, and Bobby always had a sixth sense about Ben.

They met at a company party, when John was out of town. "Bobby, please go without me and enjoy yourself," John instructed. Bobby, amused, did exactly as John told her.

Ben was also at that party, alone.

He was what people call raw-boned. Tall, with black hair and the largest, thickest fingers on the biggest hands she had ever seen, and his facial features were the same, large eyes hovering over a huge nose. His lips were thick, spreading over large teeth, and he laughed freely; a friendly laugh, a perfect companion for this uncomplicated, intelligent man.

She couldn't help herself. She thought, "Hmmm, wonder if his bobby matches the rest of him. Forgive me John, dearest, I have no evil intentions, just a natural curiosity," and she was most curious about this man who had just entered her hum-drum life—a life filled with a houseful of kids and an old man.

The two of them left the group and drifted off by themselves to the upstairs bar and for two hours sat and chatted. She learned he was a graduate of John Carroll University in Cleveland and was one of the first men in the development of plastic compounds; solely responsible for many of the patents the company held. He was married and had one daughter about Cindy Butterfly's age. At the present time, he was alone because his wife was hospitalized, a frequent occurrence.

She felt she could confide in this man, she could trust him; he was like John in many ways, only much younger.

That was several years ago and Ben had always been friendly since that time. Now here he was on the phone offering maybe more than friendship, "Bobby, please let me help you, I will be here anytime you call. Pick up the phone and I will be more than glad to help you any way possible. You know you can depend on me, don't you?"

She did.

Ben became almost like a substitute John in the next few months and years. They were friends, and Ben was her guardian and protector, always hovering over her like a huge father bear...gentle, dependable Ben. Bobby, being Bobby, always leaned on him for advice and guidance and she always knew he was just a phone call away. She could pick up the phone at any time and he would be there.

It was a wonderful rare, guilt-free relationship and both of them seemed to thrive in the knowledge of their friendship, while living separate lives. Ben had obligations, and Bobby knew that as long as those obligations were there, she could never pursue her curiosity about his physical characteristics.

Although she herself would probably never turn down the opportunity for a sexual liason, she also knew she would be involved in a fruitless dead-end affair with a married man which would never be enough, emotionally or financially. She had never washed socks without being in the will and she wasn't about to begin now.

Also, to her complete surprise and at times, consternation, Ben Morrison never pushed for more than friendship.

In retrospect, she realized that in her frantic attempt to get financial security at any expense for herself and the kids, when she married John Belk she unwittingly and blindly married a sex object. She had never been in love with him, but that old man had kept her satisfied for an unbelievable seventeen years. She hadn't needed, or looked for, a back-up man during the entire marriage. In fact, there were a couple opportunities she had taken a pass on, it was just not necessary.

She was ready now. She also realized she was middle-aged and had never been in love, not even once in her life. Love had eluded her. Further, she felt no compulsion to explore or contemplate the absence of that emotion; she only needed a sexual partner with money, lots of money, willing and able to marry her. In return, she would wash socks.

She had one more telephone call to make that day.

"Mr. Chapman? This is Bobby Belk. I would like to make an appointment to come in to see you. John passed away a couple weeks ago and I need to see you about his will that you have in your safe."

Melanie was sitting at her desk right outside Sid's office door when she transferred Bobby's call to him. She overheard the conversation, heard Sid hang up the phone, and then came that unmistakable unique cackle-laugh. She waited for the shoe thump on the desk.

Thump. She heard him laugh again, followed by another thump. Then, through the thin door that separated their offices, she heard him say, "Queenie."

"Here we go again," she whispered to Patty, and she could hardly wait until she got home to tell her husband about this one.

CHAPTER TEN

REVENGE

"Mrs. Belk, this is Nurse David from Robertson Memorial Hospital. I'm calling about your daughter, Cindy. She has been beaten quite badly and wants you to come here to…"

Bobby gasped, "What happened? How bad is she, will she be okay?"

"We think so, although she may have to spend the night here. Dr. Rizzo will talk to you when you get here."

By the time Bobby arrived at the emergency room she was shaking, and with motherly instinct she knew it was Richard. Richard, who hadn't come to the airport with Cindy; Richard, who sat in this very hospital the night Lori was born with alcohol on his breath; Richard, who tried to keep Cindy isolated from her family and all of her friends…Richard, Richard, Richard.

She couldn't hold back her tears when she saw her precious Cindy Butterfly on the bed, her face bloodied and already swollen almost beyond recognition. Her pretty blonde hair was coated with blood and there was a policeman standing over her, talking to her, taking down information. He was unsuccessfully trying to convince Cindy to file charges against her husband.

"Mrs. Steiner," he gently explained, "no one should be beaten like this. You have to protect yourself. If you won't file charges, I will write up the report anyway now, and if you change your mind, please call the station. Be careful. Next time it could be worse, and from my experience, I have observed once something like this starts, it generally does get worse. I don't want to scare you, but this type of behavior could be fatal for you. If you have children, you have to learn to protect them also."

Bobby shuddered when she heard those words. She wondered if Cindy, in her condition, understood exactly what the officer was trying to tell her.

Dr. Rizzo came and told her there may be a concussion. He had stitched up the wounds, and she could take Cindy home. "But Mrs. Belk, keep an eye on her, she needs to remain in bed and stay quiet. She should stay with you until things settle down between her and her husband."

It wasn't until the following day that Cindy Butterfly confided in her mother about Richard. He had been drinking heavily for years. Yesterday she found a picture of the nude woman and confronted him when he came home from Newman's Tavern, about seven o'clock, after his usual stopover after work.

"Who is she Richard?"

"She's just someone who works at the post office. A friend of mine gave that picture to me, I don't even know her. Sure has some big tits on her though, don't she?" Richard was weaving, obviously drunk.

"I don't believe you."

"Just gimme me the fuckin' picture, it's mine, not yours."

Cindy quickly ran into the bedroom and hid the picture before Richard managed to stagger into the room after her.

"I told you, gimme the Goddamn picture, you good-fa'-noth'n bitch!"

When Cindy refused again, Richard hit her with all his drunken might before he reeled around, left the room and sped off in his car, leaving her bloodied and gasping for breath.

"Cindy, I would like to have that picture to keep, and anyway, you don't want Lori or Jennifer getting hold of something like that."

"Mother, it's under the mattress in my bedroom. Hopefully, Richard will be at work now and you can go get it and keep it. Better yet, throw it away, destroy it, I don't ever want to lay eyes on it, ever again."

After Bobby left to look for the photograph, Cindy Butterfly had second thoughts. There were moments when she thought her mother was not quite rational. She worried Mother was coming down with the Myers' Curse like Grandpa B.T. and Grandma Marge. She heard Bobby saying something about a pact with the Devil once, and she remembered when she was a little girl, after her daddy was killed, Mother said God never heard her prayers.

Mother could be one determined, delusional woman at times. Cindy, in spite of her pain was amused, and maybe a little bit giddily philosophical, "Guess it runs in the family, heaven help us all!" She realized it had been a long day already, and she just wished she hadn't sent her mother on that errand.

At that very moment Bobby was holding the photograph, walking into the Pineville Post Office. She looked around, not knowing quite what to expect. "Well," she considered, "no pain, no gain, if she found the woman and the woman called security, she would just have to deal with it."

She thought of Margaret with her succinct language…"my shoulders are broad!"

She spotted the woman behind the second window, a good likeness to the picture. Clutching the picture she thought, "Well, here goes."

Bobby quietly approached the woman, leaned into the counter and calmly placed the photograph so that it was right side up to the woman. "I got this from Richard Steiner. I'm his mother-in-law. Do you know him?"

The woman's eyes widened briefly as she saw her nude self in the picture in a very compromising position. The picture lay there and neither Bobby nor the woman touched it. It exposed everything she had been born with—and more!

It was like a slow motion scene as she looked at the photograph and her eyes adjusted to the piece of paper lying on her counter, but actually it was just a brief second for the situation to register with the woman. She was sharp.

Just who was this woman standing at her counter? She had never seen her before and she didn't even know Richard had a wife, let alone a mother-in-law. She had never posed for this; there must have been a camera somewhere in the room. Well, whoever this lady was, she would gladly cooperate.

Her reaction was a complete surprise to Bobby, who was expecting at any moment to be set upon by a post office guard.

"I certainly can tell you all about Richard. Just wait a minute until I get off duty, and I'll be glad to tell you anything you want to know about him."

And she did.

"I met Richard about a year ago at the Whitehouse Bar in Ravenna. He told me he was single, a widower, and I believed him. At first he was a nice guy, tall, blonde and polite, then he became possessive and suspicious and one night he beat me, tied me up and threatened to kill me. He was like a Dr. Jekyll and Dr. Hyde, I couldn't believe it."

"I filed charges against him but later dropped them, but I do have a restraining order to protect myself. I've refused to see him since then. Please tell your daughter this guy is bad news, which I'm sure she already knows by now, but she needs to get away from him. Also tell her Richard won't be seeing me, ever again, I didn't know he was married. We women have to stick together."

Snafu! Snafu! When Bobby was driving back to Casement Street she became furious, and with each passing mile her anger increased. That drunken bum, how dare he touch one hair on her child's head, how dare he be unfaithful. How dare he even breathe? What a monster. She hoped he would walk in front of a semi, or he'd fall off a roof. No, that would be too quick and painless. She hoped he would drink enough booze to disintegrate his kidneys and the sooner the better. She wanted him to suffer and be dead just as surely as she wanted Jimmy Notman dead those many years ago.

"And God, I'm not praying, I'm talkin' to my new best friend, the Devil," and she was talking to her new best friend aloud, very loud, as she drove home to take care of this situation. Somebody had to do it and she would, somehow.

When she walked back into the Casement house, she was confronted by a very worried daughter. "Oh, Mother, I'm so glad you're back, you've been gone so long. Did you find the photograph?"

"Of course I did, dear. Now, don't you worry your little head about any of this one minute more; we'll take care of it one way or another. You and the girls can move back in here, there's plenty of room. Please, I beg you; don't ever go back to him, Cindy. You deserve better than this and so do the girls."

Then a determined, superstitious Bobby added, "You'll see dear, everything will work out soon, your mother has faith."

CHAPTER ELEVEN

SID

Sid Chapman stood in front of his office window on the third floor of the bank building overlooking the small oval-shaped park in downtown Pineville. He often lingered there looking out over this quaint Ohio town, thinking how he was proud to be a part of it.

Spring had arrived, and the park was outfitted in its Easter finest. There were hats of pink and white crabapple trees, dresses of purple lilac bushes, along with pink and white azaleas. The tulips looked like red and white socks hovering over shoe masses of creeping purple, blue and white flocks.

In the middle of all this finery sat the white gingerbread adorned cubicle where the bands played every Saturday night, weather permitting. At the far end of the park stood the chalk white City Hall displaying its gleaming copper dome, with the fire department conveniently housed in the rear. Located on the opposite corner sat the finest brick church in the city, with a full wall of stained glass paneled windows. This church held a collection of the oldest, most respectable Pineville families every Sunday morning.

Sid thought the city fathers of this community were ingenious engineers. By necessity, all traffic routed around this circle, showing off Pineville's finest asset, this little park, always dressed up for the appropriate season. Every driver, regardless of where he was going in town, was forced to drive around the town circle and enjoy knowing where his taxes were being spent.

Sid emitted a deep chuckle, he was in a good mood today because his client had arrived and was waiting in the reception room. She was a client long overdue. It occurred to him he was procrastinating with thoughts about his city like a little boy saving the last dab of ice cream, licking it up quickly before it melted and ran down the sides of the cone. He was standing there savoring the thought of seeing her again.

He stood at this very window several years ago when the movie crew filmed the movie "One Potato, Two Potato." Hollywood came to this sleepy Ohio town and tried to awaken its citizens and the rest of the country to bigotry and racial prejudice. The entire film had been shot in Pineville and this town center, with its unique little park, was clearly visible. He could still see the bright neon red letters of "Mahoning County National Bank", situated on the south side of the park, splashed across the large movie screen.

The film, which ended with a white mother losing custody of her child to a white ex-husband because she had married a black man, was interesting to Sid not only from the legal standpoint, but it also held a deeper significance for Sid.

Sid Chapman understood prejudice and bigotry.

His parents migrated from Poland to escape political and religious tyranny. In spite of the fact that his dad hadn't graduated from high school, nor had his mother, both did have a strong sense of survival, along with an immense dose of common sense. When the family arrived in America they were no longer the Jewish Khapman family.

Southern Ohio only knew them as the Catholic Chapman family, an honest hard-working family of six kids living on a pig farm.

All Sid could remember was poverty…and pigs. Every morning, without fail, his brother Ashley would let those damned pigs escape from the pigpen, and every morning, without fail, he would have to haul out of bed to help round up pigs. Squealing, smelling, stinking pigs, dozens of them running lose.

Sid was determined to get them all off that pig farm, even that stupid Ashley, and the only way it would happen was by education. He had big ideas with the determination to do it. If Pop could turn a Jewish Khapman into a Catholic Chapman, then Sid could manage to get a college education and a good job. This was America, and he was American and proud of it.

But before he had a chance to accomplish this almost impossible feat, fire swept through that run-down farmhouse one day when everyone was at school, and both of his parents perished in that fire.

The tragedy only made Sid more determined than ever.

He managed to get jobs for himself and his brothers, doing anything, anywhere, as long as it was honest work. He also managed to save a few dollars for college tuition to enter Kent State. In college, he and a buddy scrounged around and managed to open up a pool hall to pay for tuition and books.

He had only one goal—he would be a millionaire before he was thirty-five. No more pigs! Ever!

Then when he was a senior in college he met Evelyn, from the Sandusky area in northern Ohio, who had a father that was quite impressed with this young entrepreneur. Evelyn's father was willing to help Sid through law school and then set him up in business. Sid sealed the deal.

He married Evelyn.

It was a simple deal, and like two business partners who were financially united, they couldn't agree on anything. What little lust there had been in the beginning was soon quickly erased by arguments and temper tantrums.

Evelyn outright hated him and he readily agreed to return the sentiment.

They moved to Akron and he studied, ignoring Evelyn and all of her petty grievances. First the law degree, then a CPA degree, and from there he set up the legal practice in Pineville on the third floor of the bank building with his law partner Tony.

It was at that time he started buying junk property. Every time he would buy a piece of property he would routinely write up a 3x4 index card and file it away in his desk drawer.

In spite of all his work and education, he was considered a maverick attorney in that small community. Not one of the good-old guys in the legal network of attorneys or their smartly-clad wives opened their offices or homes to the Chapman's.

He handled trite and nasty divorce cases. He specialized in collections and bankruptcies, which also angered the local businessmen.

At times Sid would factiously grouse to himself he might as well kept that Jewish Khapman name, prejudice was prejudice in any form, anywhere, and he would have been snubbed, regardless of his name.

It was after seeing "One Potato and Two Potato" filmed in the park and he saw the movie that he became determined to do something about the black situation in Pineville. A loyal Democrat, his favorite political quote was old Harry Truman's: "The buck stops here." Sid was determined that here, in his legal office, was a small step, but he would do his part, however small.

Sid Chapman hired the first black office worker to ever work in a legal office in Pineville, over the objection of his law partner, Tony.

Within a few years most of the black community came to Sid for their legal problems, and also for loans. He loaned money for medical problems, doctor bills, and never turned down a request for educational funding. The local black families accepted Sid as one of their own, and Sid knew in his soul he certainly was one of them. He understood, and he was rarely disappointed with the results.

All the while during those years he quietly collected 3x4 cards, investing and loaning next month's income before it had actually been collected.

Sid Chapman was a gambler, a profound gambler. He made that million about twenty years ago, before he was thirty-five, all on paper, those little 3x4 index cards. As they accumulated in quantity, they also accumulated in value.

He moved from the window around to his desk. Sitting down in his comfortable big leather chair, he pulled open the second desk drawer, removed the small green index box, and unlocked it.

He quickly fanned out the deck of 3x4 index cards with the skill of a Vegas twenty-one dealer, then pulled out the rest of the remaining cards and made another fan, almost completely covering his glass-covered mahogany desk. More cards then pigs and they didn't squeal either!

Becoming satisfied looking at them and counting, he replaced the cards neatly and closed the box. He was ready for his guest.

Melanie heard the cackle and then waited for the familiar thump sound. Was that "Queenie" she heard him say behind his door? No doubt about it, someday she would write a book about this man.

She flipped the switch on the intercom to answer his call.

"Send in Mrs. Belk."

CHAPTER TWELVE

THE NEW EMPLOYEE

Sid was all business as he ushered his redheaded Queenie into his office and helped her get settled comfortably in the chair placed in front of his desk.

"Mrs. Belk, I have John's Last Will and Testament and all the necessary papers for you to sign. This shouldn't take long to file with the Probate Court here in Mahoning County and have the succession closed. I drew this will up many years ago for you I'm sure you and John spent many happy years together. I heard you and John had a boy. I'll bet that boy of yours is a teenager by now, isn't he?"

After Sid covered the important papers, had her sign on the proper lines, and tossed in a certain amount of small talk, he casually inquired about the most important thing on his mind. "Did you bring in your resume? I do have an opening in the office for a collections clerk."

He scanned the resume, knowing he would hire this woman if she couldn't type her way out of a paper bag. This was one tempting redheaded queen and he wanted her.

She was even more attractive in middle age than when he had drawn up those reciprocal wills years ago. How could any man forget this lovely queen?

Sitting across the desk from her, he eagerly wanted her now…today: right this minute, if he could have his way. He intended to get his way, because Sid Chapman was very accustomed to getting exactly what Sid Chapman wanted.

Sid never acted upon his impulses with women, employees, or clients, however, until he looked directly into their eyes. He considered the eyes the closest to the soul of the person. He would wait until they shifted their eyes and then he would have an opportunity to safely study the person.

"I see you have no college, but over the years you have worked up an impressive work record," and Sid Chapman looked directly into her eyes.

They were hazel; an odd word, for odd eyes. Brown, with little bright green flecks sprinkled around the pupils, and the brown was almost a rust color, echoing the color of her hair.

He realized he had forgotten to breathe in that short moment. These were one of the most alert pair of eyes he ever encountered, but what amazed him most was the fact she was responding his contact eye for eye. She was studying him!

He realized this was not going to be an easy or casual conquest. He was going to have to work for this one, and watch her to see if she was an intelligent as her eyes indicated. The thought was fleeting before he said, "You're hired; you can start Monday. Melanie will train you on collections."

In his most business-like manner he rose from the desk and escorted his Queenie from the office, informing both Melanie and Patty there would be three women working in the office now. Taking Bobby by the arm, Sid escorted her from the law firm office and walked her to the third floor elevator.

Melanie and Patty, now alone in the law office, both burst out in instant laughter.

"I wonder if she knows her name is Queenie?" Melanie snorted.

Patty added, "No, I wonder how long it'll take her to find out?"

CHAPTER THIRTEEN

QUEENIE

He insisted on calling her Roberta, claiming Bobby sounded like a nickname. She rather liked it. "He is the most thoughtful and observant man I've ever met," she thought one evening, as she prepared for bed.

Everyone called his law partner "Shorty" because Tony was no more than five foot, six inches tall. Not Mr. Chapman, he never called Tony by any nickname. She was sure he didn't because Mr. Chapman considered it a degrading name for Tony. Mr. Chapman seemed to have respect and empathy for everyone, including all his clients, which, Bobby observed, were mostly black, and so was Patty, his receptionist.

She liked that about him, too. In fact, there were many things she liked about Mr. Chapman after working in his office for over six months. At first, Melanie and Patty had been slow to accept her, but they finally relaxed and she became part of the office team, although she years older than either one of the other gals. She, in turn, had genuine affection for her working comrades.

She didn't agree with them, however about the cackle laugh, and the desk thump, which seemed to be the current office discussion every time a call came in to be transferred to him and his door was closed. Melanie and Patty claimed he only did that when women called. They were absolutely wrong. Well, maybe there were a few suspicious calls, but Bobby thought those two gals were just fabricating office nonsense about those calls. Harmless small talk—that's all it amounted to.

She liked and admired this man who had sprouted from a pig farm. Yes, the office gals told her that story also. There wasn't much they hadn't talked about when Mr. Chapman was in court. But she sensed they also admired this man, who gave them vacations to Vegas every year at Christmas time and was generous with bonuses.

Sid was busy in and out of court, very busy. In one of his latest deals, he acquired a large piece of business-zoned property in Pineville on a cliff overlooking the river to the south, a perfect place for his new building. He would build it with the back of the building to the river with the front overlooking the entire town of Pineville. This was going to be his town. He might currently be a good-old boy still unaccepted by the older legal network...but someday those pompous bastards down at the courthouse would have to climb up that hill and come to him!

Wryly, he wondered if he were getting old, that fifty mark had passed. His Queenie had been sitting out there in his outer office for over six months, and he was no closer to bedding her than he was the day she walked into his office over fifteen years ago. Unemotional Sid, who cared about nothing but building a financial empire and was always cavalier about who he slept with, knew this one was different. And to make matters worse, he didn't know the reason.

Sid Chapman didn't believe in soul mates. He believed in education, making money, building cities, creating a fortune. Nope, he didn't believe in soul mates, and yet he knew she sat outside his office and she would never tolerate a casual relationship.

He watched men paying attention to her. Noticing the legal book salesman brought her coffee one morning, he knew that bastard was asking her for a date. That damned sneaky over-sexed salesman. Sid never bought another book from that man, didn't return his calls, and let him sit for over an hour before he would see him: didn't want him in the office.

He was painfully aware that Ben Mitchell was her escort and spent time with the family, but Sid would have a laid bet that his Queenie never responded to Ben's sexual desires, even if Ben had any, which Sid doubted. Sid considered himself a good judge of his adversaries, both in and out of the courtroom.

It was the next July when Cleveland experienced its first race riots. Sid was prepared, his common sense told him racial havoc would be inevitable sooner or later. Hough Avenue was burning up; it seemed the entire east side of Cleveland would go up in flames.

Four people were killed all because one black man had gone into a café and asked for a glass of water. Unbelievable—four black people killed over a friggin' glass of water. Immediately crowds of black people gathered and started burning down the entire area. It was total mayhem, and alert Governor Rhodes called in fifteen hundred members of the Ohio National Guard to quell the angry residents in Cleveland's east side.

Sid Chapman placed an ad to buy property in the Cleveland Plain Dealer and his phone began ringing. People were stampeding to get out of East Cleveland and he was there to buy up that worthless property.

"Which one of you gals will go with me into East Cleveland to take pictures of some property?" He knew there would only be one volunteer when he asked.

"I'll go, Mr. Chapman, I'm not afraid to go in there, used to visit that area when I was a little girl and I'm very familiar with all the streets," came the expected answer.

As they took Route 14 through the Ohio countryside into the city, Sid politely inquired about her daughter.

Bobby responded, "She's doing well, but maybe we can talk again about her in a couple weeks, I think she wants to file for a divorce. She and my grandkids are still living with me; my big house is filled with kids again. It's rather nice."

Small talk.

"...and how's your friend, Ben, that's his name, isn't it?" Sid just couldn't help himself.

"Ben is fine, Mr. Chapman. He's married you know, his wife is in the hospital most of the time and he's really just a good friend. Honest."

Sid would have laid a Vegas bet on that one.

They exited onto Liberty Boulevard, which took them through the scenic winding park road and under the old forsythia-covered stone tunnels leading right into the Hough area, where they began seeing armed guards on every corner. Sid was beginning to doubt his judgment about bringing her along, exposing her to any possible danger.

As they wound their way through the park and onto Hough Avenue, he found himself driving right by the 79ers Café on the corner of East 79th Street and Hough Avenue, the exact place where the altercation had commenced over that glass of water.

The stench of the ugly burned buildings became almost nauseating and the city of Cleveland looked like a war zone with an armed guard standing on every corner. The streets were empty, not one black person was foolhardy enough to step out onto the sidewalk since the guards arrived.

It could have been Poland. His mind flashed back to what his parents must have experienced before they escaped to the states.

Glancing over at his passenger, he detected fear in her eyes, but he knew in spite of the fear she was with him all the way. "Guts," he thought, "she's one spunky woman", and he instinctively knew she would be the same way in bed, if he could ever manage to get her there. It was a thought he entertained daily.

He pulled his white Mustang up into a driveway in the next block and they got out to take the necessary pictures. Damn, they would have to take those pictures and get out of there quickly, because out of the corner of his eye Sid could see the young guard on the corner with his rifle lowered, watching every move they were making.

"Get in the car Roberta, quickly; we've taken all the pictures we're going to take today. I'll come back again in a few weeks," Sid instructed as he quickly helped Bobby back into his car.

"If you don't mind, Mr. Chapman, I'm going to crouch down in the seat as far as I can. I don't exactly feel like getting my head shot off today."

"Call me Sid, Queenie," the name popped out before Sid realized he had said it.

He thought her indignant reaction was fantastic: "Queenie? Queenie? Where did that come from Mr. Chapman? I know I am your employee and if you want to call me Roberta, that's okay. But Queenie, since when?"

Sid let out one of those infamous cackling laughs that Bobby loved to hear, except this time that familiar laugh irritated her; she would never be just one more sure thing in the life of Sid Chapman…never.

"Since today, cause after today, sweetie, you're my Queenie and I'm your king."

"Over my dead body, you, Mr. Chapman, are a married man, or have you forgotten?"

Sid laughed again. He was in no hurry. When the time was right, she was going to be his, because Sid Chapman always got what he wanted.

CHAPTER FOURTEEN

FIRST SNOW

Sid was having a busy summer. In addition to the ads scouting for property in Cleveland he was in the midst of arranging the erection of the office building. He contacted a geologist, who assured him the cliff, overlooking the river, was solid enough to hold the weight of a huge weighty building. Sid then contacted a local contractor for the construction.

He had an eye on the exact building he wanted.

As he rushed out of his office he told Bobby, "Common' Queenie, let's go and take some more pictures," and before she could say a word he was out the door, on the way to the elevator.

She quickly reached for the camera and her purse when she heard Melanie and Patty snickering to each other. "Now you two stop that snickering. I am going to settle this name thing once and for all." Her voice was firm and definite; this Queenie nonsense was going to stop.

"Yeah, right," quipped Melanie, "what Mr. Chapman wants around here, he always gets and we think he wants you."

"Well, missy, Mr. Chapman is going to want a long time, cause I ain't 'bout to get involved with any attorney, especially a married attorney. So you two just don't worry your pretty little heads about me, I'm old enough to take care of myself. So there." Bobby had grown quite fond of these two younger co-workers, who treated her like one of them instead of the mother she could have been to them.

As she swiftly whisked out the door with her purse and camera in hand, Melanie and Patty chorused, "Yeah, yeah, we know. We know you're old, but you're not that old."

By the time Sid pulled the car to the curb to pick up Bobby with her camera she was primed for rebuttal.

"Mr. Chapman. Once and for all, I am certainly not your Queenie. My name is not even Roberta, it is Bobby. Like it or not, my name is Bobby. That's what my grandpa named me and that's what I prefer to be called."

Sid loved this spunky woman, although he didn't know why; it was just there, a known factor, and he also loved to prod her just to see her bristle. He wondered how far he could push.

"Okay, Queenie we'll have it your way, would you prefer to be called Mrs. Belk?"

She looked him straight in the eye. "Bobby will be fine, thank you, and where are we going to take the pictures, and of what?" she asked, as she expertly inserted the film into the camera.

"We'll drive up to Mayfield Heights, just south of Cleveland. There's an office building there I want you to look at," he answered, "it's a neo-classical Greek look, three floors with four tall columns out front. I'll give the pictures to the architect and he can draw up the blueprints from them, if we decide to duplicate the structure."

"Oh, Mr. Chapman, I know the exact building you're talking about, I have admired it for years. It'll just be perfect on that hill overlooking Pineville." Bobby was immediately enthusiastic, completely forgetting she was thoroughly irritated with him a few minutes before.

Sid quickly picked up on the mood change, "Well Queenie, whoops, Roberta, if you're still at your desk tomorrow morning, and every morning for the next ten years or so, we'll share the top floor of that building. We'll be able to look down at the entire town of Pineville."

She glanced at him, "I'll be there, but please stop this Queenie stuff Mr. Chapman, I have to work in your office with the other gals, and the name really is quite embarrassing."

"Sid, call me Sid," he corrected her, then let out one of his infamous unique cackle laughs.

Toward the end of the summer he realized he had prodded her too far. He kidded her one morning about reading the comic pages in the newspaper and immediately he sensed he pushed the wrong button with her, or, as it turned out, perhaps it was the right button.

He saw that familiar determined gleam flicker through those hazel-green eyes. That fall she enrolled in night college and started attending classes, and he knew her time at home from then on was spent pouring over books.

"What are you learning in class, have you selected your major yet?" He asked her one day at the beginning of a new semester.

"Nope, too late to be a concert pianist like my mother wanted, but I'm taking a class in music theory, along with a writing course, and an American Lit course covering the Hemingway years. You know, Mr. Chapman, college to me is like a big banquet and I want to taste it all."

"Well, maybe Ben Mitchell can help you make up your mind about which way to go, you do seem to rely on his advice now and then," Sid offered dryly.

"Mr. Mitchell has been a very good friend to me and John, before he died, for a long, long time. I appreciate his interest in me and also all the help he has been to my children, Mr. Chapman. He's a married man," and noticing Sid had his arm touching hers right at that moment, "and do I have to remind you that you are married also?" She would set the record straight about that right now. Again.

That's my Queenie girl, Sid thought as he walked back into his office. Someday, someday soon she would be in his arms; just a matter of time.

She had worked for him for almost three years. In that three years Bart and Rita became a family with a couple of children, Randy graduated from River High School and had a job, and Jeff was in his first year of college.

Cindy Butterfly finally got her divorce from that monster Richard, and that jerk had taken off for California to avoid paying child support payments. Bobby wondered if her old friend the Devil had let her down, because Richard was still breathing, and she definitely wanted that useless man dead. Maybe she had lost her death powers, or maybe she needed another trip to Vegas to renew her death vows on that corner by the Flamingo Hotel.

A trip was out of the question right at the moment, but Bobby promised herself soon; maybe not 'til next year, but soon.

In the three years of her employment, she also realized she wanted to be with Mr. Chapman when he finished his building and share the top floor with him. She not only still liked the way his cackle laugh floated through the office, but she admired this man for the many humane things she saw him do, and the respectful way he always treated his clients, black or white, and his employees. She looked forward to those hours when he was in the office instead of the courtroom.

She also knew she was in love for the first time in her life.

It was the second winter since the building had been started. There were many delays with the building construction, but the contractor, who previously only erected houses, finally managed to overcome countless obstacles: supply shortages, power outages and a few idle months while he searched for competent workers.

However, the majority of the construction was completed, thank goodness, before the Ohio snow arrived, but the new building was still empty, not much more than an enclosed framework, devoid of furniture and drapes. The carpet had been laid that day, and Sid and Bobby were there to oversee the carpeting job. Bobby had just finished measuring for the drapes.

It was 5:30, late afternoon, and a light flurry of snow, the first snow of the season, had darkened the sky. The only dim light in the skeleton of the building came from quaint Pineville streetlights as they flickered on one by one, casting rays of bright yellow across the new carpet.

Bobby stood facing the large windows overlooking the streetlights, and it looked as if the city lights were exploding over the horizon. "See Mr. Chapman, Painesville is making you your own private fireworks tonight…it's your city!"

She was short and tiny and he towered over her as they looked out at dainty fresh snowflakes swirling on their way, anxiously descending over the city. He could smell the fresh floral-scented perfume she always wore, and the clean smell of her hair drifted up to his nostrils. He knew this was the moment, at last.

He put his hand gently on her shoulder, "Queenie."

She turned quickly, looked him straight into the eyes and for the first time answered to that name, "Yes, Sid?"

He quickly lowered his head and tasted her lips and she responded. Then he lowered his lips to her neckline, that inviting soft perfect spot that throbbed under her chin. She stood there in the shadows, enjoying all the tenderness he had to give, when he realized he had never made love to a woman like this before. There had been many women with every sex act possible but nothing like this, ever before. There would be plenty of time from now on to explore her body, every little inch, but right at this moment he wanted to hold her, to smell her, and simply love her. She was at last where she belonged, where she was meant to be from the very beginning.

"Queenie, I love you, you know," he whispered in her ear as he gently cradled her in his arms.

"Yes, I do know. Now just what the hell are we going to do about it?"

The roaring cackle laugh echoed through the empty building, "Well, for starters, we'll think of something, my dear Queenie."

And they did.

CHAPTER FIFTEEN
AND THEY CAME

It was a bright summer morning as Bobby sat in her private office. She swung around in her kelly-green executive chair and glanced out the big window overlooking the entire city of Pineville. She reacted quickly.

First, she buzzed Patty at the front desk, "Look busy, sweetie, sit up straight, and smile broadly, we are about to get some very important company at the Chapman Building. Today is the big day Mr. Chapman has been waiting for…for years."

She then hit the intercom system into his private office.

"Sid, darling, sit up straight dear, and look out your window, Donaldson, Wilkes, and O'Hara, the entire prestigious law firm is coming up the hill. They are coming to you!"

"Well, it's about time they came, it took long enough. I had to build a whole damned building to get them to even notice that I practice law in this town. Let them come, I'm ready. We'll blow their minds looking at my building, Queenie. Maybe they'll even want to rent one of the offices. I'll let them have one of those cheap lower floor offices, at inflated prices, of course," She could hear his cackle-laugh through the closed doors, followed by a muffled thump. She never tired of hearing it.

Sid was one satisfied man. Years, she had hung in there with him for years, never demanding, just being there, his Queenie, his helpmate. He loved her, this stubborn obstinate, determined woman.

During those years, her kids were grown, all of them married. She told him about Jeff marrying Millie last spring in Daytona Beach. Bobby called her Millie Sunshine not only because she was very blonde, but because she had brought big a ray of sunshine into their lives.

She earned her undergraduate degree with an emphasis on history and political science during those years, and she became an accomplished pianist. "For Margaret," she told him. She had shared her life with him in so many ways, always telling him about her family. He knew when her father passed away in Florida, and that her mother still lived there with Bobby's sister, Linda, in Inverness.

It was Queenie who had named the Chapman Building. She insisted, and was adamant. Springing from an immigrant family and being a first generation American he had always named his property Revolutionary War names. They were listed on the 3x4 little index cards he still kept in his middle drawer: The Trenton Building, The Brandywine Building, and The Concord Annex.

It not only satisfied his sense of patriotism about this great country where he was fortunate to live, but it was damned good business, bringing an air of respectability to his property.

He announced the new building where he would have his law office on the top floor would be called The Camden Building.

"Over my dead body," she had replied, and then went about convincing him that he was some sort of a city founding father, building this small Ohio town into a magnificent financial empire. A family place, to raise children. An all-American city that deserved his surname set in concrete on that slab to be set in front of this office building.

"Just think of it," she claimed, "always a Chapman overlooking the city of Pineville."

Sid had chuckled when she threatened to forget how to wiggle if she had to wiggle in a building named Camden, and further she informed him that his little bobby was going to get mighty lonely without that wiggle now and then.

When the doors were finally opened to the public the concrete sign on the hill outside of the three-floored, neo-classical office building proudly displayed "The Chapman Building." After all, he couldn't have his Queenie forgetting how to wiggle...and besides, his bobby wasn't **that** little!

They were happy years for Sid and Bobby. They were a team, unfortunately a daytime team.

One year they traveled to Erie, Pennsylvania where he bought her a huge executive desk to match the bright kelly-green chairs and on the way back he took her to Niagara Falls.

He asked her to marry him; "Just as soon as I make some financial arrangements," he qualified.

Then he settled the first million dollar personal case ever settled in Mahoning County for a little boy horribly burned in a car accident. Evelyn insisted they go to Europe, and he agreed, for many reasons, but mostly to prevent any further trouble from her. He wanted to keep everything smooth and quiet as possible before he carried out his future plans with his Queenie.

When he returned the kelly-green chair and her office were both empty. God knows, she had been patient enough for years; couldn't she just have waited a little longer? Didn't she understand Evelyn hadn't been a wife to him since long before that first snowfall? Didn't his queen know that? She was an intelligent woman; did he have to tell her?

It took only a couple phone calls to find her and where she was working, the new chemical plant near Pineville Township Park.

"Damn, I bet that Ben Mitchell had something to do with this."

She was gone, his Queenie. Gone, and that kelly-green chair remained empty.

CHAPTER SIXTEEN

THE CHANGE

Oh my goodness, that man had a bad temper, his bellowing voice loudly echoed over the entire plant. With a red angry face and loud voice he would curse and swear at the workers, who were doing their best to please him. The worst thing about the situation, he was the plant manager of that chemical plant, and he was her boss.

She wondered why the hell any company would put such a tyrant into a position of authority. When she first accepted the position her first thought was this man was like a mild-mannered grey-haired grandfather, with the bluest eyes she had ever seen. Within a week she discovered what farce first impressions are, when she could hear the loud swearing and cursing drifting down the hallway to her office.

She was a corporate executive secretary with her own private office; she wasn't even under the auspices of the crummy office manager that the rest of the office workers reported to. Her only immediate job was to keep Mr. Gable happy and that was impossible, although he never swore at her. But gracious, how can you respect a man that treats his plant staff in that manner?

That man had a worse temper on him than her second husband, Ted Davenport.

Unfortunately, there was something else that was changing besides her job. She was going through menopause.

She kept recalling the tranquil sight of Grandma and Grandpa Milton walking hand in hand down by the garden every evening, and it had almost become an obsession with her that she needed to find a companion. She was getting old and she didn't want to be old alone. She wanted to walk hand with hand with someone.

Why the hell had she listened to Ben when he told her waiting for Sid would be hopeless? She would surely grow old alone, and she desperately missed Sid and the law office.

That morning she had received an envelope in the mail from Sid. He actually took the time to mail a picture of her empty kelly-green executive chair sitting in front of the window that overlooked the city of Pineville…the exact spot where he had first kissed her and held her in his arms.

As she sat at her desk staring at the picture it felt as if a knife were piercing her heart. She wondered if Sid tore the wings off butterflies when he was a little boy because he certainly managed to tear off her wings with the sight of that empty green chair.

Then she thought he must be suffering also and that thought made her feel even more morose. Life had become hopeless and inconsolably lonely.

"Bobby, within six months you'll meet one of those chemical engineers up at that new plant and you'll see, you'll be in love again," Ben had predicted in trying to convince her to take a new direction in life.

She sat in her office drumming her fingers on her desk, listening to Mr. Gable shouting and swearing at one of the workers down the hall. Hell would freeze over before Ben's predictions would come true, but she wasn't about to crawl back to Sid either as long as he was still married to Evelyn. Further, she knew it was an impossibility she would ever fall in love again, what she felt for Sid was a once in a lifetime thing…if one were lucky enough.

"It's time to get practical again, Bobby," she lectured herself. She had never married for love, and although the first two times were disasters, she and John Belk certainly shared a companionship that was steady and smooth for a good many years, and in retrospect they'd been happy years too. Most of them were, anyway.

But menopause certainly signaled a definite, alarming change.

Sitting there listening to the shouting down the hall and contemplating menopausal symptoms, she glanced out the window and saw Clark Hamilton crossing the parking lot.

She watched that distinctive walk of his. He was tall and lanky, and his Abraham Lincoln legs quickly and easily covered the parking lot span. He had an odd off-kilter loping gait and his right arm always swung free with each step. Along with the industrial hard hat, he was easy to spot walking toward her office. An attractive man, or at least not unattractive anyway, she noticed.

This morning he had two hands full of reports when he stepped into her office.

"Mornin' B.J.," addressing her by the name picked up from the little copper plate on her office door, "B.J. Belk."

"Morn'n, Mr. Hamilton, how are you this morning?" she answered, still thinking she would be old and wrinkled at any minute.

"Just fine, just fine; I'm single, got the divorce yesterday."

"Oh, that's nice, or is it?"

"Very," he answered, "never going to try getting married again. Ever,"

"Great," Bobby thought, "well, so much for meeting a nice, single chemical engineer, Mr. Ben Mitchell."

She looked at Clark Hamilton again. Not bad, and she had always enjoyed a challenge, just maybe…

Just maybe she would pull out that red bra and do a little engineer fishing.

CHAPTER SEVENTEEN

THE CATCH

As Clark left her office, he thought about her. They had shared the temporary little work trailer before the new offices were set up and he often thought she was a fine-looking woman.

The heater in that trailer had to be lit every morning. Some mornings he would be deliberately late to work in order to catch her down on the floor, trying to get that heater lit, with her little butt facing the door.

Clark was always a sucker for a cute little round apple ass and B.J. certainly had one of those. Not as young as he usually preferred, but certainly well preserved for an old broad. He corrected that in his mind. B.J. wasn't a broad, she was an educated lady, hired in as an executive secretary, but she, from all appearances, had been around the block a time or two. Rumor around the plant was that she had been a mistress to one of the Pineville attorneys for at least ten or fifteen years.

Still, she was a redhead with green eyes. If she were twenty years younger he would have been on her doorstep by now.

Probably she was cold as an icebox anyway. She never wore anything sexy, always just those high-necked business dresses and suits. But still, that little round apple ass was hard to hide when she would turn around.

Forget it. He had about a half dozen young broads he was calling, he may be pushing fifty-five, but he could still handle those young ones.

He quickly dismissed the thought of her. He had a date with a new hot blonde tonight to celebrate being single again and he intended to make the most of the night.

Thank heaven for little girls, little twenty or thirty year old girls!

Still, she was an interesting looking woman; maybe he might try that sometime, when he didn't have anything better lined up.

The next morning Clark woke with a really horrendous hangover. Not exactly what he had planned, the night before he planned on waking up with a really terrific young hot blonde in his bed after a tumble in the bed sheets. He couldn't believe when she never showed. After sitting at the bar at Regel's Inn for two hours and downing about half dozen scotch and waters he finally gave up and drove back to his apartment…alone.

Hell, he was too old and tired for these young fickle blondes anyway. Would he never learn? The last wife had been that age and she lasted a whole year and half before she skipped off with her hairdresser.

Imagine, getting dumped for a damned fag hairdresser. Well, he was certainly feeling his age this morning. And his head was splitting. Damned women, damned fickle blondes; maybe he was ready for a change.

He drove into the plant parking lot and grabbed up his reports, dropping them off at B.J.'s office, "Good Mornin', B.J."

"Good morning, Mr. Hamilton," she answered.

She stood there. The dress was a black and white checkered coatdress. Severely tailored, very prim like she normally wore…a cold icebox dress. If she didn't stop dressing like that no man would ever look at her, even with the red hair, green eyes and apple ass.

But it quickly flashed across his mind that something was different this morning, something about that dress. It had a lower neckline, and as she bent over in front of him he caught a glimpse of a red lace bra.

"B. J., how would you like to go to dinner tonight with me at Regel's Inn?"

"Why Mr. Hamilton, I think that would be very nice. Yes, what a pleasant surprise, of course—I would love to spend one evening with you."

CHAPTER EIGHTEEN

A CALL FOR HELP

Don Peterson's intercom buzzed just as he was heading out of the office to go to Pineville City Hall.

"Mr. Peterson, Attorney Chapman is on line two for you."

Don, one of the new younger attorneys in Mahoning County, was acquainted with Sid, who by now had become somewhat of an area legend around the legal circles. A maverick, a risk taker who amassed a fortune buying and selling junk property before he built the big Chapman Building on the north side of Pineville.

He was also aware of some of the stories that circulated about Sid's private life and the redhead who sat in the private office on the top floor of that building.

Regardless, Don Peterson was in awe of the older man and respected his business acumen. Sid had always been cordial whenever they had faced off in the courtroom and the two of them shared a good business relationship, but they had no current cases pending.

Don wondered what Sid would be calling him for.

"Don, Mrs. Belk has stopped working for me and she now is an executive secretary to the plant manager out at that new chemical plant up in Pineville Township Park. That's really no place for her. You know, she's one hell of a legal secretary and office manager. She's been drawing up my petitions and bankruptcies for years, and she knows the collection business inside and out...," Sid was gradually leading up to the purpose of the call.

Don was a quick study. He laughed, "Sid, are you trying to tell me I need a new office manager?"

"Something like that Don, consider it a good business deal. I'll pay her wages if you will call her and make her an offer she can't refuse. If she understands one thing, it's a good salary. However, she's worth any amount and I'm willing to pay."

"As a matter of fact, I will need someone soon, guess it is common knowledge Rosie is leaving to get married," Don responded. " Listen Sid, errr...," he stammered, but just briefly, "it's really none of my business, but as long as you're calling me, just when are you going to wise up and marry that woman?"

"Just as soon as I can, Don, just as soon as I can."

Don immediately thumbed through the phone book, found the number of the chemical plant, dialed, and when the receptionist answered, he asked for Mrs. Belk.

"Mrs. Belk? This is Don Peterson. I hear through the grapevine you've left the legal business."

"Yes, Mr. Peterson, and I am beginning to regret my decision. I truly miss that type of work, and really not completely pleased with my position here," offered Bobby.

"That's why I'm calling. I am in dire need of an office manager, you may remember Rosie. She's getting married next month and has turned in her resignation. The pay is excellent and you'll have your own private office. Would you stop by next week some day and we'll talk a little more about it? Don't bother bringing your resume, I've seen you frequently in the courthouse and know you are more than qualified for the position."

Don waited.

Bobby could hear the shouting down the hall, Mr. Gable was reaming out another plant worker.

"Yes, Mr. Peterson, I believe that sounds like a great idea; would Tuesday evening about 5:30 be convenient for you?"

"Absolutely, I'll look forward to seeing you."

Don Peterson hung up the phone and redialed.

"Sid? It's all set for next Tuesday. How much are you willing to pay?"

"Anything, Peterson, just get her. And thanks, Don, I owe you one." Sid Chapman never changed. What Sid wanted he always got, one way or another, whatever it took, he would do. All he needed was a little more time.

CHAPTER NINETEEN

THE REAL REASON

Peterson was just young enough to enjoy the intrigue, he had an honest-to-goodness larger than life love story unfurling in his very office. Sid Chapman's redhead working for him, and it only took several weeks to grasp the real reason Chapman was so anxious to get Mrs. Belk out of that chemical plant.

Sid's redhead had a serious suitor, one of the engineers shipped in to work at the plant.

"Another date with Mr. Hamilton tonight, Mrs. Belk?" Don politely inquired.

"Yes, we've been dating about six or seven months now. Mr. Peterson, please call me Bobby, it would make me feel more comfortable," and she added with a soft laugh, "I've been called worse in law offices before."

Don had heard about some of the Queenie stories but he kept a straight face and offered, "Well, let's even this out, Bobby, I'm probably young enough to be your son, why don't you just call me Don while there are no clients around to hear us."

"Please…don't remind me how old I am, and thank you, I will call you Don, although it may seem strange for awhile. I hope I can live up to your expectations around here."

"You already have," Don assured her.

It was five o'clock and at that very moment Clark called, "Honey, let's have pizza and beer at your place tonight. I'll bring enough for everyone, are Cindy and the kids going to be home tonight?"

"Yep, 'fraid so, we never seem to have any privacy, do we?"

"Only at my apartment. How about that tomorrow night?" Clark suggested.

"That sounds okay to me, Clark. You get the pizza and I'll stop by and get a six-pack of beer for us, and coke and potato chips for the grandkids. We'll all play Scrabble. How's that sound to you?"

"Super," came the response, "but tomorrow night it's my apartment and we'll play scramble."

"You're impossible; you do know that, don't you?" chided Bobby, as she picked up her purse and waved goodbye to Don, who was just leaving the office.

"Lock up for the night, Bobby. I'll see you bright and early tomorrow morning."

"Boy, Sid better do something soon," he thought on his way down to his car, "going to be interesting to see how this thing works out. Give it another six months to a year, bet she marries that Hamilton guy unless Sid does something soon. In the meantime, she's been one damned good office manager."

CHAPTER TWENTY
WEDDING PLANS

He couldn't believe he had popped the question. There they were in his apartment, he had put some steaks on the grill while she prepared the salad and they spent a comfortable evening together: as usual, dinner by candlelight, complete with wine.

Maybe it was the damned wine, or maybe it was the sex, which was always very good and they were both comfortable with that also. But then at the current time he was comfortable having sex with a couple of women, because Clark always had more than one going at the same time. The trick was to keep them all separated.

They had both climaxed and were lying there talking. She smelled good, and she looked absolutely youthful and vulnerable lying there in the soft light against his spotted animal sheets. "B.J., have you ever thought about getting married again?"

It was a casual question, yet all at once it seemed to be a great idea.

Bobby answered the question directly, "Clark, I've been married too many times already, but I have only loved one man in my life. But yes, I would like a companion. I don't want to spend the rest of my life alone, how about you?"

"Same here, B.J. Would you consider marrying me? I'm being transferred to Baton Rouge, Louisiana and I think I'll really miss your little apple ass…how about it?"

Bobby thought about it a minute. Nice looking man, sex wasn't bad, his bobby was adequate, and Cindy and the girls could live in her Casement Street house. What the hell, why not?

"I may consider it, but only on two conditions. First, you buy me a concert grand piano when we get to Baton Rouge, and second, we get married in Vegas. Oh, one more thing, Clark, you must promise me you'll take me there every year on our anniversary. I want to stay at the Flamingo. In return, I promise you I'll be the best damned wife you've ever had. By the way, will I be Mrs. Hamilton number four or Mrs. Hamilton number five?"

"You've got a deal Mrs. Belk, and you'll be number five. No alimony, right, just in case it doesn't work out?" It was a counter offer.

"You got it, Mr. Hamilton. Next week, before either one of gains some sanity and changes our minds?"

"Yep," answered Clark, and the deal was sealed.

Don Peterson hated to make this telephone call, "Sid? Don here. I have some really bad news, Bobby just eloped last weekend to Las Vegas with that Hamilton guy who works at the chemical plant. She says he is being transferred to Baton Rouge soon. God, I hate to lose that woman, best office manager I've ever had. I'm really very sorry, Sid, we are both losers when she leaves."

An ashen-faced Sid was waiting at her car parked in the Pineville lot when she left the office at five o'clock.

He quickly pulled her into his arms," Why, Queenie, why? You know you don't love him, you just took the easy way out."

She felt the familiar warmth of his body; warmth she never wanted to forget because she knew this would be the last time, as she tenderly kissed him on the cheek.

"No, dear Sid, I took the only way."

CHAPTER TWENTY-ONE

THE EASY WAY?

Marriage counselor Vivian Williams, who prided herself on her ability to patch up the worst cases of dysfunctional marital relationships in the Baton Rouge area, was about to be graphic and brutally honest.

"Your marriage is like a great big gorgeous living room with piles of shit polka dotted across the carpet. It's time to clean up all that shit and move on, Bobby."

In the middle of the combined session with both Bobby and Clark Hamilton last week Vivian Williams at one point held up her hands and exclaimed, "Wait. Wait. Wait a minute. I'll be right back," and with that she had left the room. She couldn't stand one more minute of the session. Let them sit out there and argue alone, with each other.

Today she had Bobby in her office without Clark. Was the woman being deliberately dense? Couldn't she understand her husband had a sexual addiction? One of the worst cases Vivian had certainly ever witnessed.

As Bobby drove home after the session with Vivian she thought about the polka dots. Snafu! Snafu! Could nothing in her life be black and white? Why was everything gray? Gray shit. All over the place, in their living room, in the kitchen, in their four bedrooms, all over the damned place. Was she going crazy? Was she getting Alzheimer's...The Myers' Curse...like Grandpa B.T.?

Shortly after she and Clark moved to Baton Rouge he struck up a friendship with Olivia, one of the young women at the plant he worked with, and her husband Victor. Vic was out of town working every other week, leaving Olivia free to socialize. Bobby wasn't overly fond of this woman because she suspected Olivia was socializing with Clark and as it turned out her instincts were correct. She didn't trust Olivia and she sure as hell didn't trust her husband. Not for one minute.

She and Clark would go out to breakfast and Olivia just happened to show up at the restaurant on the same morning, at the same time. By herself. And they expected Bobby to think it was a coincidence? Not when it happens the third time it isn't. Apparently they thought she was stupid.

Another time, Olivia thanked Bobby for letting Clark take her to practice at the shooting range.

"I'm sorry, Olivia, Clark didn't mention to me that he's giving you shooting lessons. Are you dating my husband?"

"Oh Bobby, I'd never do that, I had no idea you didn't know we were going to the range together." In a rat's ass, Olivia was just letting Bobby know they were seeing each other and Clark wasn't telling Bobby about it.

No, Bobby, didn't care much for Twinkle Toes Olivia, a nickname Bobby had given her because of the shiny gold tennis shoes Olivia insisted upon wearing. Ironically, It occurred to her nicknaming was just another skill she picked up from Margaret.

One day she was on the phone relating new suspicions to Cindy. Clark was denying everything, of course. Maybe she was going crazy, maybe he was telling the truth, she was just imagining everything, or was she? Was it the Myers' Curse? All at once the phone went dead, utter silence.

"Cindy? Cindy? Are you still there?"

Only silence from the other end of the phone.

"Cindy?"

"Yes, Mother, I'm still here. I never thought I'd tell you this, but I know you must be told exactly how things really are. Don't believe him, Mother; you aren't getting like Grandpa B.T. and Grandma

Marge. You don't have the Myers' Curse; he tried it with me last year. It isn't your imagination."

"Cindy, dear, why didn't you tell me before?"

Cindy was clearly in tears by now on the other end of the phone, "Because I thought you were so happy at times."

Bobby quickly thought back, "Cindy, is that why you didn't want to stand beside him while we took your wedding pictures when you and Darwin got married in this house last year?"

"Yes."

"Okay, tell me all about it, I want to hear."

"Well, do you remember the night Laura and I went out? When we came in she slept in your spare bedroom and I crashed on the sofa. You and Clark were in bed. In the middle of the night he came out of your bedroom and tried to have sex with me. He wanted me to put his hand on it, kept trying to take my hand and put it on his penis. It was hard. I pushed him away and he went back to bed. Well, he came back a second time and I pushed him away again, then ran in to the bedroom with Laura."

Bobby left for Florida to think things over. She needed to talk to Linda and Margaret, needed their advice. No, she didn't want a divorce. No divorce…murder, maybe, but no divorce. No point in praying, God never heard her anyway, she just wished she could be out of this mess. Maybe he would die; his father had died at a young age. She wished him dead, fervently. Snafu! Snafu!

Margaret tried to be patient with her daughter, she genuinely tried, "Forgive him, Bobby. No one's perfect."

"I can't, and Dad never put you through this hell."

"Well, your father was no angel either. Then leave him," she said, eyeing her daughter.

Why couldn't this girl get anything right, ever? Gracious, this daughter of hers was over sixty with grown grandchildren and she still couldn't manage to get her life in order.

"I can't do that either, Mother. There are financial problems to be ironed out," Bobby replied, thoroughly miserable, and wanting some sympathy from her mother.

"Then go back to Baton Rouge and iron them out, but for Pete's sake stop this whining and mooning around. Pull up your bootstraps and deal with it. You made your bed, now lie in it. For heaven's sake, grow up!"

"Gee thanks, Mom, I'll keep that good advice in mind." How had she even imagined she would receive any empathy or sympathy from Margaret?

Linda was amused, and after Margaret went to bed that evening she asked Bobby, "Don't you miss Dad more than ever now? You should try to live with her, since that no-good gigolo she married left, she is totally impossible, Bobby. I don't know how long I'll be able to handle her. It may be necessary to put her in a home like they had to do with Grandpa B.T. You know, this has been coming on for a long time now, do you remember how she acted when Dad died?"

Bobby certainly did. The three of them had left Lyle's room to grab a sandwich and were standing in line at the hospital buffet.

"Well, I don't know what you girls are going to do after all of this is over, but I'm going to get remarried!" announced Margaret.

Bobby and Linda looked at each other and said in unison, "To whom?"

"Well, I don't know yet, but I'll find somebody and he's going to be a younger man, you can be sure of that. I'm not dumb enough to marry an old man that has to be taken care of like somebody else in this family."

Margaret then refused to return to Lyle's room, she decided to sit in the hall and that is exactly what she did when they returned upstairs.

Linda and Bobby were the only ones who heard his last feeble words, "Marge, whaaat do you wan…t, honey?" and he was dead, with his eyes open, still believing he was talking to Margaret.

An angry Bobby turned to her sister, "Don't you dare tell her what just happened, that her name was the last thing he ever said. I honestly don't know why he loved her so much. She left the room, wouldn't come in here. She's sitting out there in the hall drink'n coffee, prob'ly balancing her damned checkbook or on the phone check'n his life insurance policeees…," Bobby was so angry the last few words that had tumbled from her mouth were slurred so badly Linda could hardly understand her sister, but Linda got the drift anyway, and totally agreed.

After the funeral, Margaret immediately shopped for a husband like a renter who is looking for an apartment after receiving a three-day eviction notice and it didn't take her long to find a young man to take her to the altar. And needless to say he also took her money, then he took off, and Linda moved in to try to handle Mother.

They decided that handling Mother was beyond their ability, and so they consulted with Aunt Jane.

"Aunt Jane, do you think its Myers' Curse, she seems to be getting worse," they said.

"Oh hell no, girls, she's been that way most of her life. I've prayed and prayed for her, but it's never helped. You'll live through it; we all have, just keep a good eye on her, and leave it up to the Almighty. He'll take care of her and watch over you two also."

"Bobby, Aunt Jane can pray all she wants, but we had better try to think of something practical before its too late," advised Linda.

Bobby also knew instinctively her no-nonsense younger sister was right, there would probably have to be some decisions made soon. "Linda, I have to go back and try to work things out with Clark, but before that while I'm here, let's just scout around and check out the nursing homes and get some idea what we'll do when the time comes."

"Sounds like a good idea to me, sis. Let's do it."

She returned to Baton Rouge with more on her mind than when she left, and to make matters worse, it was open warfare with Clark from then on. Even Vivian Williams was of no help. Bobby moved into the spare bedroom and the battle lines were drawn, somewhere in the hall between the two bedrooms.

Then the letter arrived from a New Orleans' attorney. It was for Clark. What the hell was Clark doing with a New Orleans' attorney? Bobby furiously tore open the letter.

Snafu, Snafu, Snafu!

During the time she had been in Florida, Clark had driven to New Orleans and managed to get himself arrested in a black whorehouse.

No, not for screwing a resident, which he was there for and probably had already done, but the police raided the place. He had been arrested for illegally carrying a gun.

Clark always carried a gun. Their home had so many guns and ammunition in it she could have supplied World War II and had enough weapons and ammo left over for Vietnam. That cache could have blown up the entire subdivision of Wood Ridge if a match had been tossed in the wrong direction.

Then one day she found the pornography in her attic: pages torn out of magazines and carefully filed into a large volume, along with video films, dozens of them all in an insulated box so they could withstand the attic heat. It had probably taken him years to gather a collection of that magnitude.

Vivian Williams had certainly diagnosed this man correctly. She had said he would get worse as he got older and impotent, trying desperately to recapture his sexual identity and youth.

Bobby stewed. Clark was worse than Jimmy Notman had ever been. Snafu, what a mess, she wanted him gone. The fifth Mrs. Hamilton would be the last Mrs. Hamilton and where the hell was the Devil when you really needed him? Now there were two men on her hit list: Richard Steiner that good-for-nothing bum was still living in California and had never supported her grandchildren, and her sex-fiend husband, Clark Hamilton.

She needed a trip to Vegas. She wanted to stand on that corner between the Flamingo and Barbary Coast and curse Jimmy, and that slut Bonny and God again, and renew her pact with the Devil. Snafu, Snafu! She thought about Sid and cried, then got angry again. Sid had only collected 3x4 index cards, not porn. She thought about Ben Mitchell with his sterling advice and got angry. She thought about being old and became physically ill. She needed a trip to Vegas.

Then she thought about her mother's advice and decided, after three boxes of Kleenex, just to pull up her bootstraps and get to work on her marriage. Amazing how she had to wait until she was in her sixties to appreciate Margaret's sage advice.

She would make do. She hadn't picked character when she married Clark. After all, her own character wasn't so exemplary; it became eternally tarnished when she aborted Dwight David. The death wish against Jimmy sealed her fate when it was granted, and she knew she was barred from heaven when she lost her ability to pray.

She picked necessity when she married this time, and she was going to grow old with necessity. She was stuck in this faithless marriage and would live with it; perfection was just an illusion, anyway.

She was amused. Maybe she would try praying again. What the hell, it had been a long time, maybe God was ready to listen to her again. If that didn't work, her old pal the Devil always had his ears and arms wide open.

CHAPTER TWENTY-TWO

ANOTHER WRONG ONE, GOD

She would make do, and making do meant making herself look young again. Clark was fascinated with young women. Okay, she had always been vain, loved expensive clothes, and was overly concerned and proud of her appearance. She would be the first to admit she wasn't doing this completely for Clark. Being realistic, someday with a little luck she might be a lonely widow and now was no time to let her body or face go to pot.

It was the process of making herself young again that the next death occurred. Cindy Butterfly, driving her to New Orleans to have her stitches removed from the face lift, confided to Bobby how happy she and Darwin were since they married two years ago. They met during one of Cindy's visits to see Bobby and Clark. Cindy moved to Baton Rouge when they were married, leaving Lori and Jennifer in the Casement House in Pineville. The two girls, both in their early twenties were very self sufficient and actually welcomed the thought of living on their own.

"Mother he treats me so good, so different from Richard. I don't know why I ever stayed married to Richard as long as I did except he was my first love. But there are times I do miss him and think about him, in fact, quite often lately.

Bobby was alarmed. She knew it would be so easy for Cindy Butterfly to regress and see Richard again should he ever return from California. Old habits sometime never died.

"Cindy, you have got to promise me you will never go back to him or ever see him again."

Cindy Butterfly laughed, how preposterous she would ever be with Richard again, "Oh Mother, I have Darwin now."

"Cindy, dear, you never know. You just never know what the future will bring. Who would ever guess a few years ago we two Yankees would be living in Louisiana now? Unexpected things appear and lives change. Something might happen to Darwin, he might get killed. You have to promise me you'll never see that monster Richard again, no matter what happens. You have to," and Bobby's voice rose with extreme urgency.

For some reason, it was vitally important to extract a firm promise from Cindy. Right now, riding and sitting in this car. Now!

Maybe it was just the aftereffects of all the surgery, but right at moment Bobby had a most vivid premonition of death. Death, why would she think of death and Darwin? She couldn't visualize a damned prayer, but she could see the gray specter of death himself.

That conversation occurred in August and Darwin, dear, dear Darwin with the attractive little beard and those handsome straight teeth and lovely smile, who treated her daughter so lovingly, was instantly killed on the interstate in front of the Governor's Mansion in Baton Rouge, on New Year's eve.

A freak one-car accident, they were told. No one witnessed what happened and there seemed to be no explanation, but a passing bus driver saw the car crumpled against the guardrail and stopped to check. What the bus driver saw in the car was Darwin, crushed to death by the steering wheel.

The family bought burial plots in Baker, Louisiana. Bobby and Clark, Jeffery and Millie Sunshine, Cindy bought one next to Darwin, and Randy, who married Laura, a little gal he met in Baton Rouge, bought two plots for them. A family in shock and grief that quickly recognized despite good times there would eventually come a time for death and departure, and it was time to prepare for those sad future inevitabilities.

After the funeral, Bobby brought Cindy Butterfly home and put her to bed much like she did when Cindy was a little girl. Everyone was asleep for the evening or had gone home, and Bobby sat before the fireplace. The house was quiet for the night, and all she could hear was the faint sound of coals softly crackling in the darkened room.

"Damn you, God, you got the wrong one again. Can't you ever get anything right up there? Now remember, the names are Steiner and Hamilton…Steiner and Hamilton…Steiner and Hamilton. Do I have to stand on that bloody corner in Vegas to remind you?"

Then she turned off the little nightlight and walked down the hall to her own bedroom, without so much as a passing glance into Clark's room as she made her way through the hall to her own room.

CHAPTER TWENTY-THREE
HELLO GENERATION SIX

Two weeks after Darwin's funeral the entire family pitched in, helped Cindy pack up what few belongings she had in Louisiana, and moved her back to the Casement House in Pineville. Bobby made the trip to help Cindy get everything together again.

Poor Cindy Butterfly, but now this, a bigger problem, at least in Bobby's opinion, as she heard Cindy explain, "Mother, there isn't any such thing as illegitimate children anymore. Do I have to tell you that you are old fashioned? Out of date? Jennifer will just be an unwed mother."

"Am I hearing correctly," thought Bobby, "Cindy Butterfly is defending that girl after all the problem she had been?" Jennifer started being a big headache when she began skipping school in the fourth grade, and the headaches became bigger over the years.

Last year she had taken Lori's car, without permission, of course, and immediately had an accident in downtown Pineville.

She was being sued and called her Grandma Bobby for advice. "Her name is Sue Ellen and she told me her daddy is an attorney in town. We were all in court yesterday," and Jennifer continued on with the all the details, "…Mother says they can't collect…"

"Wait a minute, Jennifer, go back," Bobby interrupted, "what did you say that girl's name is again?"

"Sue Ellen, Grandma. Why?"
"And her daddy is a Pineville attorney?"
"Yes, Grandma, that's what she said."
"I'll call you back later, dear."

Bobby pulled out her old address book and looked up a name and number. At one time she would have known without the reference, but it had been a long, long time. The Myers' Curse again, she thought as she dialed.

He didn't have to ask who was calling, and she didn't have to ask for him. They knew immediately they were talking to each other, some voices remain for a lifetime.

"Sid, what the hell do you think you are doing after all we were to each other? After I came down here I rented a typewriter and worked for hours typing up labels and political pamphlets to get you elected as a state representative up there; even mailed them at my own expense. Now your daughter, Sue Ellen, is suing my granddaughter Jennifer and you are the attorney?"

"Roberta...errrr...I mean Bobby, dear, I didn't know until just this minute that girl is your granddaughter. She's blonde and tall and you're a short redhead. She must take after your daughter's husband, from that Finnish family over in Youngstown."

"My daughter's ex-husband," she corrected.

Sid continued, "She's quite beautiful, you know; a real beauty, almost as pretty as I remember her grandmother."

Bobby could feel herself softening as she always had when he pursued her. He was the only man who ever had the nerve to reach over and give her a little goose on the behind, nervy bastard! He probably never changed with age either, probably only got worse.

Hundreds of miles away, separated by years of not seeing him, and she could still feel his presence. She had been very angry with him and here he was just toying with her—again.

"Well, I just wanted you to know what you've done. I'm sure Jennifer deserves everything she gets, but damn it, what a thankless way to treat an old mistress."

"Now Queenie, you're not old. Calm down, sweetie, it's not the end of the earth."

That did it. Conversation over as far as Bobby was concerned. Just goes to show it's easier to get older than wiser she thought. When she realized she was trembling, just hearing his voice again, she couldn't hang up the phone fast enough.

Two weeks later Jennifer called, "Grandma Bobby, that girl's daddy attorney dismissed that lawsuit against me. Said the insurance company would take care of the entire matter and I probably wouldn't be able to pay anything anyway. He's really a very nice man."

"That's fine, dear. Shall we send him a sweet thank-you card?" Her voice was dripping with sarcasm.

"Oh, Grandma Bobby, be nice, you don't even know the man. Or do you?"

Now, here only two weeks since Darwin's funeral and her own daughter was telling her Jennifer is pregnant. She was about to be a great-grandmother for the first time to an illegitimate baby. A sixth generation Myers and illegitimate, how fortunate Grandpa B.T. wasn't around to witness this sorry turn of events to the Myers' family.

"Unwed mother? Unwed mother? What is that, Cindy Butterfly?" she said in response to Cindy's claim there are no illegitimate babies anymore. "Some of us may have managed to get pregnant before we got married in my day, but we always had at least one man around in the shadows willing to marry us and be a father to our baby. My first great-grandchild and it has no father? What am I going to tell your Grandmother Marge?"

She persisted, "We've never had an illegitimate baby in this family."

Cindy Butterfly, exasperated, finally faced her mother. "Well, we're going to now, and you can tell Grandma Marge anything you want, just what is she going to do about it anyway?" The discussion was over as far as Cindy was concerned.

The tense moment passed, but as much as Grandma Bobby loved those grandchildren of hers, she just didn't understand them. She just didn't.

She returned to Baton Rouge, and six months later Edwin Scott Steiner bellowed his way into the world, welcomed by Grandma Cindy and Great-Grandma Bobby. There was still no daddy in sight and Grandma Marge never said a word.

No one bothered to call Florida to tell her. "Thank goodness," Bobby said with a sigh of relief.

CHAPTER TWENTY-FOUR
THE BIG FLOOD

Within a few months after Edwin Scott was born, Clark retired from his job. All at once the house in Wood Ridge with four bedrooms, two and a half baths, the huge dining room and den, in addition to the formal living room was just too large. The maid came two times a week and even then it was difficult for Bobby to keep it dusted and cleaned.

They would have to downsize, and Bobby thought maybe a change of scenery would be best anyway. Clark was still running the roads, and she didn't know where he was or what he was doing when he drove out of their driveway. Impotent and still running the roads, where was the Devil when she needed him?

"Steiner and Hamilton," she reminded Him one day as she thought of her death-wish powers when Clark pulled out of the driveway to heaven knows where. Needless to say, Clark never kept his wedding promise to take her to Vegas every year, but she visualized that she was standing on that corner in front of the Flamingo shaking her fist at Jimmy, that blonde bitch Bonny, and demanding either God or the Devil eliminate both Richard Steiner and Clark Hamilton.

However, she did realize other than a few glitches, little things like not knowing where Clark spent his retirement days, she was relatively contented. Things could have been worse. Her kids were all grown and happily married, except for Cindy Butterfly, and even she managed to find a nice boyfriend up in Pineville.

Maybe retirement would be better also, and it seemed to be once they made the decision to sell. Clark and Bobby enjoyed looking for property and when they found the acreage sitting on the cliff overlooking the Tickfaw River they knew it would be theirs. There was a skeleton of a home already on the property that wasn't finished yet, the house had been framed in and stood on wooden piers about six feet high. They could finish the home any way they wanted to.

"We put it on the piers just in case there would be a hundred-year flood…not likely…just in case," drawled old man Conners as they signed the final sale agreement and handed him the money.

The hundred-year flood occurred about four months later, just before the Hamilton's were to move in.

The home was almost finished. Bobby wanted an open design so she could stand in the kitchen, just big enough for two people, and be able to talk to everyone in the house. She wanted a happy house, designed for entertaining the kids and grandkids. It would have one large open room accented with a spiral staircase leading to the loft. Half of the living room area would be a music room, holding her shiny black concert grand piano and there would be cathedral ceilings that seemed to soar to the heavens.

She always wanted a garden window in her kitchen. "Ain't no problem," the carpenter told her.

She always had wanted a raised corner bathrub. "Ain't no problem," the carpenter had said, and in went the tub in a special tub room.

"That little ole' carpenter can do anything," she thought, one day as she admired his work.

The cathedral ceilings were so high that Clark rented a scaffold and Bobby, deathly afraid of height, carefully crawled up the scaffold to paper the walls with bright floral pink and blue hydrangea wallpaper. Clark stood behind her to hold her and provide reassurance.

She always thought of Margaret when she wallpapered, just another thing her mother taught her that came in handy during the last few years.

It had been raining most of the day when the first flood occurred just as Bobby was finishing up last minute painting before they could move in. She had their two dogs, Chance and Pansy, with her and when she went to leave for the day the water had already filled up the gully between the house and the upper paved road.

There was no way to get out. The water started getting higher and higher and the sun was descending. No electricity. No heat. No telephone. No food, except for a little dog food she had thought to bring to the house a few days before. She was completely cut off from the world, but thank goodness she did at least have a flashlight in the car.

She went out to get the flashlight and discovered the water was almost completely surrounding the house so she moved the car to the highest point on the lot, hoping it wouldn't be swept away by the water. As she eyed the depth of the water already, and it was still rising, she became apprehensive. Not one to scare easily, she was, she admitted to herself, very frightened.

This was definitely a new experience for a Baton Rouge subdivision woman.

A few hours later she heard a horn from the distance and saw light signals from the area of the paved road. Clark had come to investigate when she hadn't returned home for the evening. She signaled back with the flashlight she found in the car.

Then she heard a motor boat in the distance and when it grew near she saw the men tying up the boat to her back porch. The water was at least two feet high under the house.

"No, I won't leave my dogs," she said, adamantly.

"Ma'm if you won't leave 'em, then we'll hafta go back and get your husband and bring 'm here to stay with you, and bring in supplies. Can't leave you here, it's cold and you have no food," the young fireman said, too polite to add, "and you're an old woman."

Bobby thought about it for a few minutes. She judged the water was dangerous across the gully and she didn't want to risk the lives of about a half dozen people.

"I promise you, Mizz Hamilton, your animals will be safe. I'm familiar with this flooding back here and it won't get in the house. The water always goes down as fast as it comes up; it'll be gone in a couple days. Your dogs will be dry and safe and there seems to be plenty of food for them. We just can't leave you here 'lone, however."

She permitted them to slip the life jacket around her and fasten it securely. When she got into the boat one of the firemen pushed her down to the bottom of the boat and they revved up the engine, and started out across the murky dark gully.

They were about half way to safety when she heard the fireman say, "Watch out for that snake!" Too late, the snake hit the propeller engine, becoming entwined, then somehow flipping off the engine into the boat, hitting Bobby's leg. One of the men quickly bent down, yanking it away from her leg, but in the excitement the boat engine sputtered and died. Now they were drifting dangerously close to the tree stumps that were on both sides of the gully with no power. Bobby closed her eyes and caught her breath. Still feeling the snake on her leg, although by now they had managed to throw the snake overboard, she fervently wished she hadn't lost communication with God years ago.

What would they do if that motor didn't start again? What would they do? She knew. They would hit those tree stumps and it would all be over. They would certainly drown.

Thank goodness the dogs were left safely in the house, they would be okay, but would she and these brave firemen?

The fireman tried to fire up the motor again. Nothing. And then again, and still nothing. All the thing did was just sputter and they were quickly drifting into the stump area. By some miracle it sputtered about the fourth time, roared to life, and quickly transported them to the other side of the treacherous black water.

She stepped out of the boat into the arms of a very relieved waiting husband, and thought to herself, "This is one hellofa way to build togetherness."

"Oh, my goodness, that was a terrible experience," she said to the crowd of neighbors who by this time had gathered to see the rescue. "Just how often does this happen anyway?"

Before anyone else could answer her question some little kid piped up "Every time it rains ma'am."

"Beautiful," she thought, "It takes a kid to tell the truth."

It was two days before Clark waded in through the cold water to rescue the dogs.

So much for Louisiana hundred-year floods on the banks of the Tickfaw River, they came every year.

CHAPTER TWENTY-FIVE

THE MYERS' CURSE

The Hamilton's had just moved into the Elephant House overlooking the Tickfaw River when Linda called. She was desperate.

"Bobby, I'm afraid of her, she's out of control. I was in the bathroom and she took the broom and tried to break down the door with it. She screamed at me that she was going to give all her money away, she said she's gonna find someone and give it to them to take care of her; we will never have a penny of it."

"Well, Linda she's already done that one with the last guy she married and that's about all she's got left anyway, a penny, but I'll come right away. We'll have to do something, she might hurt herself. Or you."

"Yeah, she keeps taking the car and getting lost. Last week she got all the way up the coast and then couldn't find her way home. Someone called me from a Burger King and I had to go get her."

"I'll drive over right away. Just give me a day to get a few things wrapped up around here for Clark," and Bobby left for Daytona Beach the next morning.

"Push the dresser against the door, Bobby," Linda instructed as they prepared to go to bed. They were both frightened of this woman, their mother, who by now seemed like a stranger. That first night they made the decision to contact the state to have Margaret tested because she refused go to an assisted living facility voluntarily, insisting the girls were just trying to get her money.

The following day the nicest young fellow showed up at the door to interview all of them. As Bobby and Linda sat on the front steps of the home and listened, the fellow had a long talk with Margaret.

Margaret was at her best. She talked and told the young man she wanted to get her own apartment in Inverness, where she lived at one time before she and Linda moved to Daytona Beach. She said her daughters were just imagining things; she was perfectly capable of taking care of herself.

Linda and Bobby could see them sitting in the living room having a pleasant chat for about two hours before he came outside to where they were waiting. Absolutely charmed by this little old lady, he told them, "Your mother's fine, absolutely nothing wrong with her, ladies. There's no way you can force her into going into a either a nursing home or an assisted living home unless she's willing to admit herself," and he handed them a business card before getting in his car and backing out of the driveway.

An angry Margaret, now aware that her daughters had called in the state, came to the front screen door where Linda and Bobby sat on the steps and told them, "Well, you girls have really done it now. I'm going to Inverness to live." With those words, Margaret turned and immediately rushed out the backdoor, quickly entered her car and drove off.

They couldn't believe what had just happened. Where did Margaret find the keys? They had hidden them earlier in the day so that she wouldn't take the car out and get lost again.

It wasn't more than half an hour later the phone rang.

"Mizz Milton, this is Daytona Beach Police Department. We're hold'n your mother here at the station. She was picked up confused and lost by the interstate. Didn't know where she was, but she said she was try'n to get to Inverness. You'll haveta come down t' the station and pick her up and arrange to get her car, its still sit'n up by the interstate where we found her."

The week had taken it toll, and Linda had reached the point of total exasperation. In her school teacher tone of voice she said firmly, "No,

I won't come. Your state social worker left here about a half hour ago and told us my mother is just fine, that she's capable of taking care of herself. I suggest you either bring her home, or take her back and put her in her car and send her home. I have rescued her for the last time," she informed the officer and hung up the phone.

A disgusted, tired and thoroughly defeated Linda quickly picked up her own car keys and announced, "I'm going to work, Bobby, I'll see you later."

Bobby got in her own car and drove down to the beach. She sat there for maybe two hours listening to the gulls and soaking up the peaceful and soothing sound of the waves. She watched them foam up, and fan out as they rushed toward the pristine sandy beach, where the foam would turn into little bubbles and then recede, only to be gobbled up by the next incoming wave.

She listened to a child's laughter which drifted from further down the beach, and she watched the patrol cars making their usual rounds, driving through the hardened pathways made in the sand.

"What are we going to do with Mom?" she asked herself. Margaret kept getting lost, she let her food burn on the stove, it wasn't safe to leave her home alone and they were actually afraid of her. She seemed to hate them. To make the situation worse, no one seemed to recognize the change in Margaret, although an alert pharmacist had called Linda when Margaret claimed her daughters were trying to poison her with prescription medicine.

It would be just a matter of time until Margaret hurt herself or someone else. They certainly had to get something done before that happened.

Refreshed somewhat by the salty air and the beach sounds, she slowly drove back to the house, which she thought would be empty.

It wasn't, and most alarming, there were two police cars parked at the curb!

There they sat. Margaret and Martha Beard, a police social worker, were engaged in light conversation, sitting in Margaret's white wicker chairs in the sunroom. Martha started to speak, "Are you Margaret's daughter Bobby? Bobby, you know Florida has these elder laws to protect our older residents…"

"Good gracious," thought Bobby quickly, "this woman is going to read me my rights!"

Bobby could hear Martha continuing, "…now Margaret and I were just having a conversation about changing her lifestyle and going into a nursing home, but she doesn't think she would like to live in a home…"

At that very moment Linda barged into the room in response to a frantic call at work from a neighbor concerned about the police cars out front.

"I don't know what you are charging my sister with, but whatever it is, you can put me on the list too and take both of us in with you," she informed Martha Beard.

Martha was a pro; she had been around these situations before in this state where dealing with Alzheimer's patients is an everyday event. Family members were often the first ones to realize the onset of this horrendous disease before it becomes apparent to friends and neighbors, or even social workers and doctors.

She had been engaged in conversation with Margaret for over an hour waiting for Margaret's daughters to come home and she knew exactly how to handle the situation.

She went to the phone and quietly and competently made all the arrangements, while Margaret sat in her white wicker chair in the sunroom, thoroughly convinced she had made a new friend; a friend who wouldn't listen to "those girls" of hers.

Margaret walked past them, preceding Martha and the deputy, and over her shoulder she informed them, "You'll see, they can give me any damned test they have and I'll pass every one of them. There's nothing wrong with me…it's you girls. Your dad will be thoroughly ashamed of you, just wait until I tell him."

Margaret had forgotten Lyle died several years ago.

That week they made arrangements for their mother to live at an assisted living home. She had her own apartment, complete with kitchenette, cable television, maid service, a nurse on call, all of her meals delivered to her room, planned recreational activities, and a beauty shop on the premises.

Margaret refused to talk to them.

CHAPTER TWENTY-SIX
RETURN TO VEGAS

Cindy Butterfly sat before the mirror, checking for wrinkles. They must be there somewhere, because she would soon be celebrating her forty-ninth birthday next month.

Impossible, how did she let that happen? Laying down the hand mirror and stepping over in front of the full-length mirror reaffirmed she was still tiny and blonde and everything on her nude body looked great. Except the double chin, she unhappily observed. Maybe she should visit Mother's favorite plastic surgeon, the one that did her last face lift in Baton Rouge.

She picked up the hand mirror lying on the dresser again and flipped it to the magnifying side for the closest possible inspection. Looking at her image, she convinced herself, regardless of her impending birthday, she had more grandchildren than wrinkles. Thank goodness.

First Jennifer had Eddie, and then Lori married and produced two more children, Hannah and Ethan, making three grandchildren.

Her biggest concern at the moment was not really about getting old and having wrinkles, it was Grandma Bobby and her complete inability to understand Lori and Jennifer. If it wasn't complaining about illegitimate children it was something else.

During her mother's last visit it was something else. "Mother, it isn't really important anyway what they name those babies, you know they love you too," Cindy claimed, patiently attempting to smooth out Grandma Bobby's temper again about Lori and Jennifer. A temper that could go up and down like fresh coffee pushing itself into the top of the little glass dome of the coffee pot in the kitchen.

She thought her mother might be getting the Myers' curse because she could really be impossible sometimes. But maybe, just maybe, this time she had a good valid point this time. However Cindy Butterfly wasn't about to let that coffee pot boil over either, she would just try to turn down the heat a little, as if that were possible.

Remembering the arguments over Dwight David with Margaret, Bobby knew it shouldn't really matter what those grandchildren of hers named their children. It was totally their business.

However, did they have to be named after Richard's parents? Those girls only vaguely remembered their father, still hiding out in California, and they rarely saw his parents.

First it was Edwin Scott after Richard's father, a wonderful human being, and now Hannah Elizabeth named after Richard's mother, a fine woman, but just what the hell did either of them ever do for those grandchildren and great-grandchildren of hers? They had never sent one thin dime when their worthless son refused to pay child support—ever.

They had never worked and handed over piano money, earned by sitting at the keyboard teaching piano lessons, they had never rescued Lori's cat and taken it to the vet. And paid for the vet bill! They hadn't sewn every precious little dress for Lori when she entered kindergarten.

Cindy Butterfly was tempted to add, "And etcetera, etcetera, and etcetera."

"...and exactly what the hell is all this living together without being married that everyone seems to be doing nowadays?" Bobby continued.

Cindy Butterfly almost wished Mother would return to the name complaining.

"If they aren't good enough to marry, Cindy Butterfly, then they aren't good enough to live with. Think about that!" After about four move-ins and move-outs and payments of money to move-outs, Cindy had learned her lesson. On that score, her mother was absolutely right.

But Lori and Jennifer never seemed to get the message. It seemed like a passing parade through their apartments. Lori's husband found another woman on the computer and deserted the family two months after Ethan had been born. Since then, there had been one tattooed idiot after the other camping out at Lori's house like it was Yellowstone Park.

Grandma Bobby didn't mince any unnecessary words about her granddaughters' lifestyles, "Dumb, dumb, dumb," and Cindy Butterfly agreed, although she privately admitted sometimes she dreaded her mother's audible opinions.

Then one day Cindy could barely stifle a laugh. Jennifer had accused her Grandma Bobby of being old-fashioned.

"Old fashioned? Old fashioned? Well, girlie just let me tell you a few..."

Thank goodness, Hannah had rushed into the room with a skinned knee right at that moment, because Cindy knew her mother could indeed tell those grandchildren of hers a few stories.

"Some things in families need to be kept secret," Cindy thought, although Cindy Butterfly would have loved to have heard the rest of that sentence.

The phone rang, bringing Cindy back to the present, thinking again about her birthday wrinkles. It was Bobby calling; they must be having ESP thinking about each other.

"Cindy Butterfly your Aunt Linda and I have just put Grandma Marge in an assisted living home. It has been one horrible week, and I am going back to the Elephant House. After I get the house straightened up and check with Clark, how would you like to have a terrific birthday present?"

"Sounds super to me Mother, what do you have in mind?"

"How would you like a trip to Las Vegas? I haven't been there since my honeymoon with Clark over ten years ago. They've just opened up the Venetian and the Aladdin has been demolished and rebuilt and I've never even seen a picture of the new Paris casino. Which one would you like to go to?"

Cindy Butterfly was thrilled, "Oh Mother, I just saw the Aladdin on the travel channel last week and they showed all the shops there, about a hundred of them all in a circle, with a small stream running through the area. Let's go there!"

"Great. I'll get on the computer and make all the arrangements and you apply for vacation time. We'll make it next month."

It was about time they had a little fun in their lives, and besides, she wanted to check out that corner between the Flamingo and Barbary Coast once again, it had been much too long. Where the hell were her death wish powers when she really needed them?

The next month they both flew into McCarren Airport, Cindy on a direct flight from Cleveland, and Bobby from New Orleans with a connection through Phoenix, and they met at the baggage section of Southwest Airlines and took a Bell Transportation bus to the Aladdin.

"Cindy Butterfly, did you bring all your glitzy clothes to wear?" As they unpacked they were like two sisters and friends planning the next few days. First, they made reservations to see Tom Jones at the MGM the next evening, then called Paris to have dinner at the top of the Eiffel Tower that evening. After that, they hiked up the strip to the Bellagio, where they admired the botanical gardens.

"Mother, this has got to be the most beautiful view in Las Vegas," Cindy Butterfly told her as they sat at the top of the Eiffel Tower having dinner that evening. Across the street they could see the fountains of the Bellagio. The colorful lighted water sprays would dance into the black sky, fall back, and repeat the dance again and again—thousands and thousands of water sprays putting on their spectacular show for the evening dinner guests at the top of the Eiffel Tower.

The next morning they arose early and ate breakfast at one of the restaurants along the inside street of the Aladdin before they went shopping. "This place has got to be a shopper's oasis for a shopoholic," Cindy Butterfly declared.

With their feet aching from hours of walking through different stores, they found a bench along the inside stream of water which runs along the sidewalk stores at the Aladdin. From the distance they distinctly heard a rumble coming from the convincingly inside painted sky above. The rumble became louder, and then a streak of lightening came from somewhere before the rain began falling in front of them. Not on them, in front of them.

Little raindrops made indentations in the water, starting out small, and then becoming large drops of rain strongly beating into the water as the thunderstorm was overhead; and becoming small droplets again as the storm receded and passed over them, gradually fading away completely as the thunderstorm moved away into the distance.

What a show, what a delightful, marvelous make-believe neon city this city had become. Bobby couldn't help but recall the strip the first time she and John came here on their honeymoon. About the only thing here then was Caesar's palace and the Flamingo area, the old MGM was about the last casino on the strip then. At that place now sits Harrah's, and the strip has probably tripled in length since those days.

"Cindy, they've installed a computerized canopy over the entire length of Fremont Street downtown and the shows run at least until midnight. After we see Tom Jones tonight, let's hop a strip bus and go down and see it."

"Sounds great to me. First, let's go back to our room and get some rest before we go to the show tonight. My feet are aching and I'm tired," she said, faking a moan.

"You're tired, it's just your forty-ninth birthday, do you realize what that makes me? At least fifty," Bobby winked and nudged her daughter.

The phone in the room was ringing as they entered their room.

"Richard is dying in Los Angeles. His kidneys have given out and he's asking for you, Cindy," came the ominous report.

Cindy slowly hung up the phone, shared the message with her mother and asked, "Mother, should I go? He's asking for me, he was my first love, and he's Lori and Jennifer's daddy. Should I go?"

Bobby thought for what seemed to be a long time, this was a crucial scene, she didn't want to encourage her daughter to face the heartbreak of seeing Richard on any deathbed, but she knew she had to be very careful what she said at this particular moment. One of those critical times so important she knew she would have to measure every word very carefully.

"Cindy, honey, this must be your decision. I will lend you the money if you need it. Los Angeles isn't too far away; you would have time to go if you want to. But I won't enable you, I expect you to pay me back. If you want to spend your birthday going to see Richard I will understand. It's your decision, dear."

It seemed like an eternity, an absolute eternity—must have been at least two minutes, an eternity. Cindy sat. Bobby sat, realizing she had been holding her breath. She exhaled and took another breath, then another.

"I've decided, Mother. Come on, let's go down to the casino, I feel lucky. Then we'll come back and get gussied up to see Tom Jones."

Bobby thought luck had nothing to do with it. Her best friend the Devil had finally taken care of the situation.

The next morning, while an exhausted Cindy Butterfly was still sleeping, Bobby got up, dressed and quietly slipped out of the door.

She headed straight to that familiar corner.

It was an older, slightly calmer woman that stood in that spot on the sidewalk in front of the Flamingo Casino this morning. Was she talking to the Devil or God? She didn't know, maybe both.

"Well, it's about time. I know you still can't hear me God, even if you do actually exist somewhere, but I'm here to remind you, it is Steiner and Hamilton, both of them. And it took long enough, I must say. Just what is keeping you so busy up there nowadays anyway? And Jimmy, by the way, I still hate your guts, along with that blonde bitch you were with when you bled to death on this very spot."

As Bobby opened the door, Cindy sat up in bed, "Mother, where did you go?"

"Just out for our breakfast, dear. Here, I brought you some coffee and doughnuts. It's a lovely sunny Nevada day out there, let's go shopping again."

On the way home sitting in the Phoenix airport between connections to New Orleans all at once she had a thunderbolt thought. "Oh dear, I forgot to say which Hamilton I wanted dead when I was standing in front of the Flamingo, Mr. or Mrs. Well, I'll just have to wait and leave it up to destiny."

CHAPTER TWENTY-SEVEN

OF COURSE HE'S A MAN

She was faintly aware the young nurse was praying over her.

"Don't bother doin' that, honey, ain't gonna do any good at all, the doors of heaven were closed to me years ago. What I need is a drink. A bottle of beer, and I'm cold," Bobby mumbled, as she shivered under the warm hospital blanket.

Nurse Tara took another soft blanket and covered her patient, "Mizz Hamilton, you're fine. Let me just put this ice cube in your mouth and you'll feel better. Your doctor will be in to see you as soon as we can get you out of the recovery room and into your room."

Bobby's mouth felt like it was on fire. Good. Worry about the mouth while she felt to see how much of her breast was still there. Anger, she was just damned angry, angry enough to swear—repeatedly. That first damned doctor was going to cut it off and suggested she have both of them removed as a preventative, just in case the other breast would develop a lump in the future.

Dr. Jeb had set up the surgery for the following week. During that week she enlightened herself about breast cancer; made trips to the American Cancer Association; got on the telephone; and talked to other women. The morning of the surgery, to the consternation of two doctors, an anesthesiologist and probably a few surgical nurses, she cancelled it.

And she changed doctors.

Dr. Jeb Robinson actually breathed a sigh of relief, "What a difficult patient. First patient who had ever told him if it were his...what did she call it? Bobby that was it...anyway, if it was his bobby instead of her boob, it would come off an inch at a time and that's the way her breast was coming off...an inch at a time!" Thinking about what an inch would mean to him, he figured maybe she had a good point, and referred her to another surgeon as she requested.

However, "stage two" cancer was nothing to fool around with. He also tried to console her, "With God's help, you will be fine."

Normally the "God's help" routine helped calm down his patients, but Mrs. Hamilton had actually laughed and said, "To hell with this God thing, just refer me to a surgeon who will do want I want done."

So she changed doctors, found one who would take out only as much as necessary. She also called Dr. Teague in Baton Rouge and explained to him she was having breast surgery, would he come in and do a little happy surgery for her also at the same time?

"Doc, if I have to have this damned surgery done, do something to make me feel good, something to live for. How about just a light little chemical peel around the mouth to remove the wrinkles—you know, the ones creeping out from my lip line. Sometimes my lipstick absolutely looks like hell after a few hours."

Doctor Teague, overlooking his patient's curse words, agreed the peel would be a simple procedure and he would arrange to be present at the breast surgery to do the cosmetic work. He felt some women handle life and death situations differently and this was one woman who obviously hadn't spent her life praying when cussing could handle her problems.

As she lay there with her mouth on fire, she quit thinking about the damned breast which was bound up and thought about her mouth instead. After they took her into her room she asked the nurse for a mirror.

"Now Mizz Hamilton, there's plenty of time for that tomorrow."

"I don't want 'tomorrow', I want to know now, hand me a damned mirror like I asked you so I can see what I look like today. And I'm still cold and thirsty. Now, I said," she snapped.

Dumb. Dumb. That's what she had been. She knew she should have been more specific when she stood on that corner and death-wished a Hamilton. What did He need up there, a woman secretary to keep things straight?

These new women libbers tried to say God was a woman, but she knew God was a man the way He screwed things up most of the time and never listened. If He were up there at all, of course He was a man. All these damned prayers people send to him and he's probably up there reading The Wall Street Journal, smoking a cigar, having a scotch and soda and pinching Mrs. Claus on the ass.

Well, if she were going to die at least she was going to make sure she would be a well-dressed beautiful corpse, with two breasts in the proper place, if possible. She envisioned Clark standing over her casket and wished she had more lovers to mourn over her. She thought about Sid.

Surely Ben Mitchell will be there, although in truth he had actually never been her lover. She could almost hear Ben saying, "She is beautiful, isn't she? She looks so natural, like she's just sleeping." She wondered to herself if everyone facing the big C had these hallucinations, or if it were only unique with the Myers' women.

Clark was there when the doctor came in and told them the news, although Bobby already knew it was more than the breast by the abundance of the bandages under her arm. The cancer had spread to the lymph nodes under her left arm and he had removed them, but she still had her breast, the doctor had removed only a little pie shape where the lump had been. Thank goodness she found a doctor who would follow her instructions, instead of offering radical surgery and blessings.

She would need six weeks of daily x-ray treatment, followed by chemotherapy.

Aunt Jane showed up as if by magic, like she had when that no-good Jimmy had left her pregnant and alone when he ran off with that slut Bonnie. This time Aunt Jane was again there to take care of her, driving her every day to get the x-ray treatment.

Her doctor was amused, "I'll have to take care good of you because I'll hear from Aunt Jane if I let anything happen to you."

She had three handsome, young doctors taking care of her: first the surgeon Dr. Adams, then Dr. Jackson the x-ray doctor from Mary Bird Perkins in Baton Rouge, and finally the oncologist, who advised her, "We're going to be seeing each other for a long time, Mrs. Hamilton."

And so they did. It took about a year of treatment. A year of taking a bath every evening because she was afraid of dying during the night and she wanted to be clean for the undertaker.

Also a year of more surgery, a device in her chest to receive the chemo drugs because her veins couldn't take the endless needle insertions.

She found herself separating her mind from her body, a body that betrayed and disappointed her, a useless body she would soon be discarding. During the nights and days after the chemo treatments when she felt she had to get out of her painful, itchy, crawling skin to escape the effects of the drugs, she would put her mind in a safe soft: in the back of her bedroom closet, that blue and white papered bedroom that held her girlhood memories.

Never one to bother with figures and counting, she had time to reflect now "Aunt Jane, this horrible "feeling" lasts for three or four days after each treatment. I will need at least nine treatments over the next months, that adds up to about an entire month that I might as well be dead. I'll never make it. Repeating Snafu, even a cuss word now and then, doesn't even help anymore."

"Now Baby, you're going to make it, the Good Lord looks over us, you just keep praying, and block those cuss words from your mind. He listens; He'll be there for you. You do pray, don't you? If not, 'bout time you sit your little self down and git busy."

During the final months Bobby found she was too weak to walk. She crocheted, she made colorful afghans. When her hair fell out from the chemo, she bought three wigs, different colors, and found out that blondes really don't have more fun. Not this one anyway, this was no fun, just pure hell with an indefinite ending.

It took about another year until things were almost normal, although she still needed a cart to lean on for support when grocery shopping. Her body simply ran out of gas at the most inconvenient times.

Now there was another problem, she had one breast that had been reduced and then shrunk up by the x-ray treatment. The thing looked small and perky like it had when she was a teenager.

The other one looked larger, older and drooped, and as she stood before the mirror she looked at her two mismatched disparate breasts and decided it was time for another visit to Dr. Teague. She hoped just maybe she would live long enough to have someone enjoy looking at them.

Dr. Teague knew his patient had beaten the cancer because her vocabulary had improved. She hadn't uttered one cuss word; so far, anyway. Sitting in the corner of the little cubicle studying the position and condition of both breasts, he was positively upbeat, "I can help you, Mrs. Hamilton, I can reduce your right breast and lift it to match the one that had the cancer. You will have a pair of matching breasts again."

"More surgery to produce a beautiful pair of matching breasts, with no one to look at them," she mused. Clark, who had become increasingly more distant during the entire ordeal, no longer was interested in physical contact. Bobby reminded herself someday to write a book about the effect breast surgery has on personal relationships and how many men simply cannot cope with the problem and walk away.

"Mrs. Hamilton, Dr. Adams wants to speak to you," and Dr. Adams came on the phone and told her his plan for making a short television film about his cancer patients and would she permit them to film her to show what could be done with breast cancer patients? It would be shown on a local television channel. Of course her face would not be shown and she would not be identified.

"Dr. Adams, too bad you can't show it all because Dr. Teague not only has done a great job on my breasts, but he has also taken care of my face and stomach at various times. That man is a genius, just like you. I've been fortunate to have had the best doctors."

As she and Aunt Jane watched the program showing her breasts on television one evening, Bobby forgot about her longstanding lack of communication with the Almighty, if he actually existed, and before she could stop herself she sent up a little prayer of thanks. Maybe Aunt Jane was there beside her for more than one reason.

However, upon further consideration she figured even if by some remote possibility the door to heaven was slightly ajar, being a man, He probably was still too busy with the stock market report and his scotch and water to hear her.

CHAPTER TWENTY-EIGHT

MR. HAMILTON

Clark rose from bed that morning and checked the river from the living room window of the Elephant House as he did routinely every day. The day was overcast and dingy gray and he wondered if there was a storm brewing down in the gulf. It looked like that kind of a sky.

Climbing slowly up the black metal winding stairs was an onerous chore, but he wanted to make some more ammunition. He worried what B.J. would do with all this stuff after he was gone and instructed her, "B.J., call the Baton Rouge Police Department and donate all these bullets and equipment to them if anything should happen to me." He knew when he told her that something was going to happen to him. He was going to die, and soon. How ironic, two years ago he thought he would be burying Bobby, and now instead it would be the other way around.

He'd had surgery and one round of chemo and six months later the doctor told him another round of chemo would be useless.

She had taken care of him during those months. All in all, true to her word she had been a good wife to him, except she could be a real corker at times. When she decided to be unhappy, everybody was unhappy. Clark chuckled, remembering a few of the times.

When she found out about Olivia and that New Orleans problem she had gone ballistic and he was afraid she would never come back. They didn't mean anything to him, and he told her that, but she never seemed understand.

She told him then if she ever caught him cheating again and he wouldn't stay home and stop running the roads, he would have to buy her a mink coat and fork over money for a plastic surgeon.

He didn't want her to leave. That fur coat hung upstairs and she sure looked young, she must have had two or three facelifts and a tummy tuck trying to keep herself looking young and pretty. Along with the furs and facelifts over the years, he also paid off with a couple diamond rings that were almost as big as the headlights on that little red sports car she drove. Just to keep her happy.

She was sure one expensive woman, but she had kept her word to him; she had been a good wife, in spite her temper outbursts.

After he made a few more bullets, he was so exhausted he could hardly wind his way back down the stairway and walk outside to the hammock by the river. He layed there and listened to the wood sounds from one direction and the sound of bubbling water from the Tickfaw coming from the other direction. Guess if one had to die this was an ideal spot; B.J. had picked a good name for the place when she called it the Elephant House, a place to die.

Bobby was watching Clark lying in the hammock. She felt guilty. She wished he could go out and get in his truck and run the roads again. All that didn't seem to matter anymore; in the scheme of things it just wasn't important. When the doctor came into the waiting room after the operation and told her there was nothing they could do, her tears were genuine and surfaced immediately.

Well, hadn't she wished him dead? Yes, she couldn't deny it, yet when it appeared to become a reality she fervently wanted to take back her wish. A retraction was too late. She should have known better to death-wish after the others met such terrible fates—all dead, after angry words and deliberate vengeful prayers. Only the Devil could have heard and given deliverance to her evil requests.

There were six people dead, including her three husbands, that bitch Bonny, Cindy's Darwin and that good-for-nothing drunkard Richard.

The only one she hadn't wished dead was dear Darwin, but even that was brought on by her premonition. Now Clark was dying.

So she guiltily nursed him during this last year after the surgery and through the chemo ordeal, and today Hospice arrived for the first time.

Randy also arrived early in the day to rearrange the living room, making room for the hospital bed. Waiting for the Hospice nurse, she couldn't help but think their living room looked like a miniature hospital scene.

She slept on the sofa that night and every night for the next three weeks. He became so uncomfortable she called the Hospice nurse, who promptly arrived and put a catheter in Clark.

He kept calling to Bobby and trying to get out of bed to go to the bathroom. She stood next to the bed while he leaned on her, all six foot-four inches of that big frame. Ordinarily, still weak from her own cancer problems, she wouldn't have been able to support that weight, but tonight, for some unexplainable reason, it was possible.

About four in the morning she heard him gasp. She went to him immediately as he gasped one more, then he was still. No last words, no expression or pain. He never woke up, he just died, right at that moment. He never told her goodbye, he was just gone, sleeping peacefully forever. "The finality of death," she thought, "at least this one was a peaceful one; no violence or pools of blood left to dry on a Vegas street; a decapitated, blood-dripping ripped head flying through the air; or an open-eyed corpse with a hard bobby in one hand, grasping his chest with the other hand, while waiting to have sex with me."

She audibly shuddered from all the dark thoughts swirling around in her mind as she dialed the hospital nurse, who arrived almost immediately. Bobby wondered if she was losing track of time, because the nurse couldn't have had enough time to get there so soon, but there she was, at the door.

As the two of them waited for the hearse to arrive, Bobby insisted they dress Clark. Because the nurse put the catheter in the night before, Clark had on only a t-shirt covering the upper section of his body, and she knew he would be embarrassed if his genitals were showing when they took him to the funeral home.

Tears appeared on her cheeks, quickly brushed away, as they pulled his pants up over those long, lifeless legs. She drifted back in time and thought about how those Abraham Lincoln legs had loped over the chemical plant parking lot the first day he spotted that red bra and asked her for a date.

She could feel the tears welling up somewhere in her throat and eyes again. Where were those damned things coming from anyway, she wondered. He certainly hadn't been any Prince Charming during the entire marriage, and in truth she hadn't been any pillar of purity either. Nothing to mourn over, for sure, this marriage of convenience wrought with mutual infidelity, and she wouldn't. Not for long anyway, if these damned tears would just stop.

"I know you must feel real bad, Mizz Bobby, but he is really in a better place you know," the observant nurse consoled from the opposite side of the bed, as they pulled up his long-legged pants.

Bobby hesitated for a minute as she wiped away the pesky tears…Oh, she wasn't so sure, then she replied, "You are probably right, Ann. Nobody's perfect, and he was probably a lot better than most, but he was sure one heck of a rascal at times."

Days after the funeral Cindy Butterfly looked at her mother and asked, "Mother, did you ever really love him?"

"Maybe, sometimes, he was a difficult man to love. Let's just say he wasn't the love of my life, but I loved him about the same as the other three."

CHAPTER TWENTY-NINE
THE WIDOW HAMILTON

Sure enough, it didn't take long. In Tangipahoa Parish, Louisiana, good news always travels slowly in the Daily Star Newspaper, but bad news and gossip travel through backyards along fences and across phone lines faster than horny squirrels.

Within six months after Clark's death one of those horny squirrels now sat at her dinner table looking at Bobby like she was a sweet-meat pecan morsel. Good, faithful friend Ben Mitchell here, all the way from Ohio. Not only sitting at her table, but now a widower—and talking marriage.

"I told my friends in Ohio when I left them that I may be married by the time I get back," big rugged, gentle Ben beamed. But she learned within twenty-four hours after his arrival of his impotency and she was downright disappointed, thinking at last she would find out if his bobby matched his hands, fingers, nose, and his teeth. It was a curiosity she never confirmed in the past.

Nature could be cruel, how well she knew, and she immediately felt like stomping her feet like a spoiled child over the whole damned situation. Impotent indeed! She wasn't wasting her time on any man who could only offer her Sunday afternoon hand-in-hand Grandma and Grandpa Milton garden strolls, she needed a man with all his hardware functioning.

"Ben, I love you dearly, you have been the best friend a woman could ever hope for, but you know what happens to all my husbands, don't you? They die, my friend, and I just couldn't bear losing you."

"Might be worth the risk, Bobby," but the subject of marriage went no further, although she did agree to return to Ohio with him for a visit. She stayed at the Casement House with Cindy Butterfly, having no desire to share a bed with Ben and trying to cope with a limp bobby.

But their lifelong platonic friendship overcame any lack of sexual activity and they continued to share a comfortable companionship that only develops through time and tenacity. One Sunday afternoon they drove south out of Pineville to scenic Worship Lane, winding through overhanging green arbors, under a covered bridge, and along a little sparkling-clean Ohio creek. It was genuinely nice to again share this carefree friendship with Ben, whom she had known so well for so many years.

"Ben I think this is the road where Sid bought that farm. I never saw it, but one time after I moved to Baton Rouge, when he was running for that political office, I typed up campaign material and mailed it to Worship Lane."

"You did, didn't you?" Ben asked.

Confused, Bobby questioned, "Did what, Ben?"

"Like the name of this road, you did worship him, didn't you? I have regretted many times advising you to leave him. You know he did actually divorce that wife of his a few years after you left Ohio. He never remarried, always claimed you'd come back someday. If I have regrets about you, it's because I regret giving you that wrong advice," admitted her friend.

"I didn't know Ben, but that's all in the past now, isn't it? And I made my own decisions. Forget it, my dear friend. We all made it through, we survived the best we knew how, didn't we, and we are all still here, aren't we?"

They sure were; Ben couldn't believe his eyes. Standing right there in a circular driveway was, unmistakably, Sid Chapman. A bit grayer, slightly bent over, but still a tall sturdy, rather stocky, handsome gentleman. "Bobby, look, you won't believe this, there's Sid, let's stop to see him."

"No, no, Ben, that was a long time ago, I don't want to see him, don't want to know what he's doing, I just want to remember him like he was." If she were admitting the truth, she didn't want to see him then have to leave him, it didn't matter how many intervening years. "Maybe he won't know me either, I am older, Ben."

"Aren't we all, and I don't know what you've done to yourself, but you are like fine wine dear, you have grown better with age," assured her best friend.

Before she could object again, they were in the driveway, and Ben had quickly exited the car, walked up the driveway and was shaking Sid's hand. Still sitting in the car, she thought "What the hell will I do now?" She realized she was visibly trembling.

"It certainly has been a long time, hasn't it, Ben?" Then Sid went direct to the obvious question, "Do you ever see or hear from her now? Someone told me she's a widow again; haven't heard from her since I dismissed a lawsuit against her granddaughter few years ago," Sid laughed, "She was sure upset over that one. She got that way once in awhile, you know."

"Yeah, I know. In many ways I knew her better and understood her better than you did." Ben motioned toward the car. "Look in the car, Sid."

Sid didn't bother to respond to Ben's claim about his Queenie, he considered his old rival a milksop, who didn't have the guts to lay claim to this woman. When his eyes followed Sid's motion to the car he saw her and immediately headed toward her. Two pairs of eyes adjusted to almost fifteen years of change, important years that transport people from middle to old age. Appearances can change radically during those particular ages. Through the open window she could see Sid pause as he walked up to the car.

"Maybe he doesn't recognize me. Oh, he still looks like my handsome Sid," she quickly observed. Why had she given up, not waited, went to work at the chemical plant and married Clark all those years ago. Why?

He made his decision quickly. He was a big man, still strong even in advanced years, and he yanked open the door and effortlessly lifted her up into his arms and kissed her—an urgent, hungry kiss. He wanted to devour this woman, she was his at last, there would be no more waiting. Sid Chapman, who always got what he wanted, was ready to take what had always been his, from the very beginning.

Her white hat with the orange ribbon that matched her suit tilted, sliding to the back of her head, and between the movement of the hat and Sid's impulsive, unexpected greeting she didn't respond to his kiss.

Sid stepped back, looked into her eyes, those hazel-green eyes that he dreamed about so many times lately. He pulled her closer, until he could feel the beating of her heart and the warmth of her body, and kissed her again –this time, a slow, tender kiss.

The first snow, he had waited a long time for the first snow. It may be summertime in Ohio, but in his arms he held his Queenie and as he felt her respond to his kiss they were standing overlooking the city once more, and he was tenderly kissing her while the first snow drifted over the city. The years had melted away, he had his Queenie once again.

"Queenie, you were the love of my life and you just didn't know it."

When Ben saw the second kiss he quickly decided reminiscing with Sid was definitely not a wise maneuver on his part, he should have listened to Bobby and not stopped. "Good Lord, after all these years, who would have guessed?" he thought.

He quickly followed Sid down the driveway to the car and announced, "Bobby, we should be getting back to Pineville, you know Cindy's expecting us for dinner this evening," and before Sid could object, Ben had taken control of the situation. He shook Sid's hand, bundled Bobby in the car, and they were gone.

In the car, Ben glanced over at Bobby and saw her pull out a Kleenex and dab at tears in her eyes. He heard her softly whisper only one sentence "If only he said that years ago."

CHAPTER THIRTY
THE LAST GOODBYE

Sid Chapman watched Ben help Bobby into the big Chrysler town car. Of course, Ben would be driving a town car. Ben would have the most expensive, the best of everything and he would also have his Queenie.

Always the best, she has been, from the time he first layed eyes on her when she was the very pregnant Mrs. Belk. He often wished that baby belonged to him, but the timing was wrong. The timing during those years was always wrong, impossibly inconvenient, and she slipped away from him.

Today was also a most inconvenient time.

Just been last week Dr. Rutherford told him, "Sid, please sit down, I have the results of your tests here."

A short six months, if he were lucky. Now just what the hell do you do in a short six months that you haven't done in almost eighty years?

"Go after her Sid," he told himself, but the thought was fleeting, quickly rejected by Sid's common sense when he thought about the reality of his illness, and what lie ahead in the next few months.

Sid knew it would be the last time he would ever see her, kiss her and hold her in his arms. There would never be any more first snows. As he watched that town car carrying her away with Ben, he knew Ben would take care of her and that's the way it should be.

He turned and looked at his farmhouse, a large white peeling structure with gray bare spots eaten into the siding. Discarded junk and road-weary tires lay in huge piles at the front near the road waiting to be collected, and the grass hadn't been mowed for weeks. Out back of the house stood the run-down shabby barn, now almost empty, sheltering only a few cows, a couple horses...and pigs.

The Chapman building sold a couple years ago and the new owners replaced the concrete sign with a modern neon sign which read "The United Building." There would be no Chapman overlooking the city of Pineville, now or ever again.

Sid took a long thoughtful look at what he had today, a bereft old man whose tired eyes now focused clearly on this farm, and he could see it was identical to that stench-filled pig farm where his parents burned to death in southern Ohio.

He had only his memories, and he suddenly realized those were the most precious possessions he would ever have, the 3x4 index cards were absolutely useless where he was going.

He closed his eyes and promised his Queenie he would see her in her dreams and hold her in his arms again.

"Someday, very soon."

CHAPTER THIRTY-ONE

AND THE RAINS CAME

"Good Lord, Almighty," she thought as she drove through sheets of rain toward Inverness. Linda's call had been desperate, and Bobby immediately drove to New Orleans; she checked her car in at the USA Parking across the street from the New Orleans airport; hopped a plane to Tampa; and rented a car there. Now she was about twenty miles from Inverness, driving through unbelievable weather. Old cliché, she thought, but it never rains, it pours: first the obit, now her mother.

She had received the obituary in the mail from Ben, along with a short note. Also enclosed was a short letter to Ben written in Sid's unmistakable handwriting, "Ben, take care of her for me. She will always be mine."

Ben had written in his letter, "Dearest Bobby, I received this about a week ago from Sid, he must have written it just before he died. Don't you think it's about time we made us permanent? Think it over and call me." He signed it, "All my love, forever and ever. Ben."

Her Sid was gone, they would have never another first snow, and that was the very reason he hadn't stopped her that day, or called her later. She understood now. He was gone.

Now she also understood why he appeared in her dreams. Just like clockwork, it was about twice a week and he would be there, holding her gently in his arms and kissing her, calling her Queenie. At times she would wake up, then try to go back to sleep, because she knew he would be there waiting for her. He was the only one that ever came to see her in her dreams; he was always with her, forever in her heart and soul, a part of her, never to be forgotten.

But Sid was dead and Ben was living. All at once, she visualized herself and Ben walking hand in hand like Grandma and Grandpa Milton. It seemed to all fall in place. Her best friend Ben, would always be there for her, and Sid knew that. "Why has it taken me so long? How could I have been so blind?" she asked herself.

She immediately went to the phone to give Ben her answer, but before she could dial the phone rang, and it was a frantic Linda calling from Florida.

Margaret had fallen, broken her hip and shoulder and the doctors worked on her for hours. "Bobby, because of her age, they don't give us much hope. Now she is just lying there and something has happened to her mind, and her vital signs as poor. I think she's dying, Bobby," a tearful Linda reported, "and she is saying your name over and over and something else, she keeps babbling about a man called Dwight David. Who is he; did Mom ever have a lover, someone she never told us about? Whoever it is, she's sure in a lot of pain over it."

"I don't want to see her die in this kind of pain, crying for something or someone we don't even know about," Linda said. She could hardly get to the last of her sentence, giving Bobby time to make a decision.

"Linda, that's something that happened a long time ago, when you were a little girl. Get hold of a priest and have him meet me at the hospital tomorrow, about noon, if possible. I'll be right there, there's something I have to take care of for her."

"Bobby, what on earth are you talking about, have you gotten the Myers' Curse, she's never been a Catholic. What the hell is going on?" Linda asked, demanding an answer, and one that Bobby conveniently overlooked before saying goodbye.

When Linda met her at the door the next day, she was full of questions as she hugged her rain-soaked sister.

Shaking off the water accumulated from the car to the house, Bobby gasped, "Lordy, what a trip, if I didn't know better, I would think I was driving through the first bands of a hurricane."

"You did, Bobby. You got here just in time; they shut down the Tampa airport about a half hour ago. I'm a Floridian with plenty of hurricane experience under my belt, and I would be willing to bet the damned thing will go your way, you'll be glad I called you to come here before this is all over."

"Great, what stupid woman's name are they calling this one?"

"Katrina."

CHAPTER THIRTY-TWO

FOR THEY WILL SEE GOD

"Linda, we don't have time to worry about the weather right at the moment, how is Mom, and did you get a priest to meet us tomorrow at the hospital?" Inquired Bobby, not waiting for any answers before she asked, "And do you think she will last one more day, just how bad is she?"

Tears welled up in Linda's eyes, "Not good, Bobby. What's going on, will you tell me what's going on, who's this Dwight David? And why a priest, she isn't a Catholic!"

"Well she is now. I knew what happened when I was sixteen always preyed on her mind, I know it has mine, and I'm going to bring her relief about it any way I can. At this point she doesn't know she isn't a Catholic, and I think she'll respond to a priest. It may not do any good in the eyes of the Catholic Church, but in the eyes of God and in her mind it may bring some peace. I owe her that much, Linda. It was all entirely my fault."

"My God, Bobby, Dad must be rolling over in his grave, you doing this. But I agree, if it will help, do whatever you want. I feel so sorry for her just lying there calling your name over and over and that Dwight David, whoever he is. She keeps asking for him. By the way, you still haven't told me what this is all about," Linda immediately pulled out a cigarette, lit up, sat down and waited for an answer.

"You know what? If you don't stop smoking those things I'll have to call a priest for you. I'll tell you later, I just can't go into it right at the moment. Let's go to the hospital and at least hold her hand. I don't want her to be alone."

"If you wait a minute until I smoke this cigarette we'll go now. I talked to the hospital and they say there is a Father Leigh that makes evening rounds there and we can catch him this evening. He's expecting us in about an hour. It's all set, let's go and get this over with, whatever you plan to do. But believe me; you have some tall explaining to do afterwards."

When they arrived at the hospital Father Leigh was waiting for them, "Mrs. Hamilton and Miss Milton? I've been in to see your mother, Margaret. I waited to administer the Last Rites until you arrived, but she does seem to be failing quickly."

Deciding this was Bobby's idea, Linda couldn't bring herself to go in the room. and went to the lounge to wait until the priest was finished. She definitely needed another cigarette, and her mind was full of questions for her sister.

Bobby extracted a piece of typewritten paper from her purse. She wasn't taking any chances, she knew she would never remember the prayer, she still couldn't remember any prayers. "Father Leigh, would it be alright if I read the Act of Contrition for my Mother? She may hear it and understand, we don't know, do we? But just in case. And I would rather read it aloud for her."

"Mrs. Hamilton, it really isn't necessary, but I think it would be perfectly alright for you to do that for your mother, God does move in mysterious ways, doesn't he, maybe she will understand, and I am sure He will," an assuring Father Leigh was studying the face of this woman standing there with a typewritten Act of Contrition in her hands asking this unusual request. This was one of the first prayers a Catholic child learns, this woman couldn't possibly be what she claimed to be.

They stood beside Margaret's bed and Bobby heard Margaret faintly repeating Dwight David, Dwight David, over and over and over again.

"Mom, I love you. This is Bobby, I'm here, and Father Leigh is with me, and I'm going to read a little prayer with you. If you are able, listen and try to repeat it with me."

She gently placed her mother's hand in her own and slowly read, "Bless me Father, for I have sinned. Many years ago we took the life of Dwight David before he had the chance to breathe. Oh my God, I am heartily sorry I have offended thee and I detest all my sins because I fear the loss of heaven and the pains of hell, but most of all because I have offended you, My God, who are all good and deserving of all my love. I firmly resolve with the help of thy grace to confess my sins, amend my life and do penance," and as Bobby read the last line Father Jacobs joined in and they both prayed together, "Oh Dear God, look down on us and take Margaret into your arms and welcome her into heaven. Amen."

Although Margaret couldn't repeat any of the prayer, she ceased the mumbled chanting and appeared to become quietly peaceful as Father Leigh made the sign of the cross and then read some scripture. He placed his hand on Margaret's forehead, prayed over oil, and anointed her forehead and her frail hands. He then said a prayer for Margaret and invited Bobby to say the Lord's Prayer with him.

For the first time since that day she fell to her knees and discovered she couldn't pray, after Jimmy got killed, she was able to recite the Lord's Prayer with Father Leigh. Astonishingly, she felt a peace spreading within her soul.

With tears in her eyes, Bobby thanked the priest, who put an understanding hand on her shoulder. "Mrs. Hamilton, I am not quite sure you have been entirely candid with me, this does seems to be a bit unusual, but we can only pray that your mother will be welcomed into God's arms and you yourself, reading the Act of Contrition, will receive relief from whatever it is that is bothering your soul."

"I won't inquire further what your standing with the church is, I will only say God bless you, and God be with you and forgive you your sins, and you can be sure your precious little Dwight David has been in God's hands these many years. You and Margaret will be united with him someday," and the old priest, who had seen and heard almost all of mankind's venial and mortal sins in their quest for survival and eternal peace, made the sign of the cross over Bobby and quietly left the room.

She sat down beside her mother and held her frail white hand. She had probably fooled no one, the priest or certainly not God in heaven. It didn't concern her. Margaret herself was at peace. She knew her mother would die with inner peace, her senile mind at last released from that mortal sin, committed so many years ago.

She sobbed to this inert old woman lying quietly in the bed, "Mom, I'm sorry for all the rotten things I've put you through. I'm sorry for getting pregnant when I was sixteen, I'm sorry I put you through Dwight David, sorry I yelled at you for other unimportant things. I'm sorry I criticized you for not staying in the room when Dad died. I know now you couldn't bear to watch him die, and I'm truly sorry I never told you that your name was the last thing he ever said. Mom, I'm sorry I was angry and wrote to Dear Abby when you buried Dad on my birthday and didn't speak to you all those years after you married that guy. You just didn't want to be alone, I understand that now."

"Oh Mom, I know now you did the best you knew how to at the time and I do love you with all my heart. I always have."

Linda quietly entered the room and was standing beside her sister. Sobbing, they clung together as Margaret slowly and peacefully slipped away into God's arms a few hours later. She was at last united with Lyle and Dwight David in heaven.

The next day after they left the funeral home to make all the final arrangements, Linda demanded an explanation.

"Dwight David was my baby, Linda and why Catholic? Well, when I was going with Ted, the priest baptized me, and I never told anyone I was baptized Catholic because of Dad. After he died it had been so many years…and I never truly repented, never could bring myself to confess about Dwight David, I cursed God and never found peace in my soul…" .and her voice trailed off as she haltingly told her sister the rest of the story. She told it all: about the pact with the Devil, the Jimmy death wish, her trips to Vegas, all the other deaths brought about by her death wishes, and her belief in her own Vegas destiny.

Practical schoolteacher-trained Linda listened quietly to her sobbing older sister and fervently hoped her own tears weren't visibly evident when she said, "Oh goodness, Bobby, I wish I had a buck for every sin I've committed. Wow, I've had my share of those! For Pete's sake, if you want to be a Catholic, do it. You just confessed to me, and you know, in essence you also confessed to Father Leigh. He must have known; I'll bet he blessed you…Didn't he?"

"By the way, about those husbands of yours, I might have wished a couple of them dead too, or would have taken care of it myself. Sure glad I never had one of those buggers. Anyway, I'm absolutely positive you don't possess any death-wish powers or pact with the old Devil himself. There is such a thing as coincidence, you know. Lighten up, let's go get a cup of coffee and I need another cigarette, now!

"And also, don't be taking any more trips to Vegas, at least until you get this religion stuff squared away."

CHAPTER THIRTY-THREE

PRAYERS

The two women welcomed Margaret's friends at the funeral, and after the funeral arrangements were made to fly the casket to the family cemetery in Ohio. They immediately left for Ohio, where they would put the casket in the ground, and Margaret would lie in peace next to Lyle for all eternity. It was an onerous final task to be taken care of, the one all children know in their hearts will one day sadly arrive.

They reached the Casement house tired and hungry, met by Cindy Butterfly who anxiously waited at the door. First she gave them a good meal and then the good news; she knew they could use some happy thoughts.

"Mother, Ernie and I are getting married at Christmas in that old church in the vineyard near Lake Erie. We're planning just a small wedding with family, and we want all the music to be Italian love songs. My friend Ann has agreed to sing and I want you to play the piano for the ceremony and reception afterwards."

"Oh, Cindy Butterfly, what wonderful, wonderful news, your Aunt Linda and I won't miss that for anything, we'll be here rain or shine, and so will be your brothers, along with Laura and Millie Sunshine. You can count on us, I promise."

But the news wasn't all good, Cindy reported that Randy called and told her they were evacuating their home in Slidell, before Katrina arrived. As Linda predicted, the killer storm took aim at the Gulf Coast.

"Cindy, some of the neighbors are staying, they seem to think the dirt embankments around the subdivision will hold, they always have in the past. But this is going to be a big one, and Laura and I aren't going to chance it. Tell Mother when she arrives that we are heading to the Elephant House, it's on stilts and a little further north. Maybe we'll be safer than in Slidell, and we'll ride out the storm there. Hopefully, it won't be as bad as they predict; most often they aren't." Randy tried to sound upbeat.

She was concerned for her brother, "Randy, please be careful and call me after it's over, or while it's passing, if you can."

"Will do, love you Sis."

Margaret was buried on August 29th, 2005, a day that changed thousands of lives forever. Katrina arrived at New Orleans and the entire Gulf Coast area. They never received that phone call from Randy and Laura, either during or after the killer hurricane passed quickly through on its destructive way to the northeast.

They tried in vain to reach them by phone and e-mail and never left the television, watching in horror as CNN's Anderson Cooper reported from the area. There was one quick glimpse, showing Randy and Laura's neighborhood with people standing on roofs begging to be rescued. One of the residents had put a large American flag on a rooftop as they waited vainly for the helicopters and boats to rescue them.

"Oh, my dear God, I pray they got out, I pray they are at the Elephant House and none of those trees come crashing down on that," and pray she did, "Oh God, I hope you can hear me today, it's for my children, God, and all those poor people there," and she said a long prayer, ending with the Lord's Prayer. All at once she realized she was able to say it without reading, she knew the prayer, it was back in her mind!

That night before retiring, an old woman with a young face knelt before her bed like a child and reverently recited the Lord's Prayer again, by heart and with all of her heart. Then, dutifully remembering Margaret's instructions, she gave an amused chuckle as she signed herself and repeated, "Now I lay me down to sleep, I pray the Lord my soul to keep. Amen."

As she got in bed and pulled up the covers she heard Margaret again, "Sleep tight and don't let the bedbugs bite!"

CHAPTER THIRTY-FOUR

KATRINA—PAST HELL

With his normal bravado quickly collapsing, Randy sat in the car holding a sobbing Laura in his arms as they looked at what used to be their home.

"Oh Randy, our wedding pictures, my grandmother's dishes, our jewelry, our new bedroom set…all gone, there's nothing left. Oh, my God, Randy, I feel like I'm going to throw up, this can't be happening, we're having a nightmare."

"Laura, honey, those are only things. We're fortunate we got out, that we left, look around, see the holes in the roofs? People chopped their way through them trying to get away from the water. Honey, we'll go buy that camp in back of the Elephant House, Mother shouldn't be living way up there on the river by herself anyway. Please don't cry Laura, everything'll be okay. You'll see. Now, let's go check on your sister, see if we can find her."

As they drove through the neighborhoods in Slidell, they realized the terror Katrina had brought. Homes sat there unoccupied, homes they could see through from front doors clear through to the back doors, open spaces, homes with their entire guts scooped out, like one guts a fish and all that remains is a little meat with the skin around the empty carcass.

It had been two weeks, and there was still no power at the Elephant House and no way to call or contact anyone outside this living hell to tell them they survived. He knew everyone in Ohio and Florida was worried about them, but there was just no way to contact anyone.

He was glad Mother wasn't here to live through the ordeal, but he wasn't sure exactly where she had gone. The last he had heard, Grandma Marge passed away. Then the power went off, and the telephone lost the dial tone, even before Katrina arrived. His guess was that they had gone to Ohio to bury Grandma. Mother was better there, or anywhere else for that matter, than here.

Surrounded by a sea of debris and lumber piled up five to six feet high, they attempted to find Laura's sister's home. In some areas the houses were empty black skeletons surrounded by walls of broken lumber and bits of furniture. In the more fortunate areas, bright blue plastic tarps, provided by Fema, already covered shells of the empty houses. They looked like large elevated blue swimming pools.

Abandoned cars were everywhere, Karina had picked them up, casually tossing them like grains of rice after a wedding.

The majority of the homes were now just a pile of rubble and broken timbers, nothing left to even look like what once had been a home, echoing children's laughter; and churches amid the rubble that no longer held congregations, hosted weddings or funerals or provided refuge. The buildings were all gone, along with the people.

Katrina was not selective in her destruction. She cared not whether she killed a house, woman, man, child or pets and livestock. She was a killer that the Gulf Shores had not seen since Camille.

Most of the streets were impassable, but Randy and Laura finally wove their way to her sister's home. Although there were very few people around, in the front yard midst the rubble stood ten men in a circle holding hands, looking as if they were playing a ring-around-the-rosy game.

As Randy and Laura drew closer they realized this was no child's game, these men were holding hands and praying.

"We're from a church in New Jersey, we're the helping hands of God, here to gut out houses or do anything possible to help. We've also brought dogs and checking the houses for bodies," explained one man.

The men went on to give Randy the news that the hurricane had decimated almost the entire Gulf Coast area, including Biloxi, Pascagoula, Gulfport, Bay St. Louis, and Pass Christian. The levees in Slidell had not only been engulfed, but also the levies in New Orleans had been breached and New Orleans was under water. The coastal casinos were either damaged beyond immediate repair or gone, taken by the tremendous surge from the gulf.

One kind soul gave Laura and Randy a battery-powered radio so they could listen to the up-dated news when they returned home. Communication was at a premium, as was gas and food.

Inquiring about Laura's sister and her husband, no one knew where they were, many evacuees had been taken to Houston, or anywhere in the states that would take the homeless. Laura became frantic once more.

"Laura, honey, we'll just go back to the Elephant House and wait. You'll see, they'll be okay," he vaguely was aware of repeating himself as he continued, "they'll be okay…and so will we, honey. It surely won't be long before we get the power back on. and maybe telephone service. The cell phone service should be restored soon; I'm certain that will be the first to come back. Honey, please don't cry, we're okay. We made it past hell, we've survived Katrina."

CHAPTER THIRTY-FIVE

RITA, THE UNINVITED GUEST THAT STAYED

In Ohio, the two sisters had a sad parting. They hadn't heard from Randy and Laura, and didn't know where they were, or even whether the Elephant House was still intact. Linda left for Florida, she needed to get back because school would be starting soon, and Bobby opted to stay with Cindy at the Casement House in Pineville.

"I'll see you in December at Cindy's wedding," Linda reassured them.

With a heavy heart, she watched Linda leave without her. It would be useless to go back to Florida with her. There was just no way for her to get from Florida to Louisiana because the I-10 Biloxi bridge was out that spanned the gulf and there was no way for traffic to get through with the bridge gone. They saw it on CNN. Bobby was sure she was receiving more news that those poor people in Louisiana.

Further, all buses were cancelled between Florida and Louisiana, no way across the southern states that way, either. She couldn't fly home, The New Orleans airport was closed and in all probability I-10 was also impassable between the airport and the Elephant House north of Hammond.

She was forced to stay put in Ohio with Cindy, Jeff and Sunshine Millie and wait for news. What a miserable, futile exile, she desperately wanted to be home.

Days of sending out e-mails with the hope someone would be able to get back in touch, but no response from anybody, absolutely no response. The wait was horrific, until a few long days later the phone finally rang, and it was Randy.

Thank the good Lord, they were okay, God must have heard her prayers. The road leading back to the Elephant House was obstructed with fallen trees and rubbish, but all the neighbors had pitched in with power saws to get to Randy and Laura. Many homes, trees and fences were down around the area, but they were safe, and plans were made for Jeff and Millie Sunshine to bring Bobby back, once the power was restored at the house.

"Randy, you didn't tell her about our home in Slidell," a storm-wearing Laura told him as he hung up the phone.

"There's plenty of time to go into that after they get home, Laura. The important thing is we're okay and we can live here with Mom until we decide what to do. In the meantime, let's go check out that cabin down the lane. I think there's a terrific view of the river from there," he said, still attempting to be upbeat.

A week later, Jeff, Millie Sunshine and Bobby arrived from Ohio and everyone pitched in and worked, trying to clear out the remaining trees and debris. Then the astonishing news came from the weather bureau. Another hurricane was on the way—another lady, this one named Rita.

"Mom, this doesn't look as bad as Katrina, and you've got Randy and Laura here. Millie and I had better get out and go back to go Ohio while we can. I need to get back to work and we can't risk being stranded in Louisiana. We'll call tonight on the way home," Jeff promised, and they left the morning of September 23rd.

On September 24th Hurricane Rita arrived in Louisiana and she lingered. The power went out in the Elephant House again, immediately. Katrina had rushed through the month before, quickly and savagely destroying everything within her greedy grasp, but Rita stayed and stayed like an atrocious, obnoxious, unwelcome guest.

"You know, sometimes even an invited guest begins to smell like bad fish after three days, and we sure didn't invite this one!" claimed Randy the second day, as they sat listening to the winds and watching the trees bend under hurricane-grey skies.

They were huddled in the candle-lit living room when the big tree that hovered over the house crashed, limbs breaking and splintering, all around the house. Rita was going to have the last word before she moved on to Texas.

It was dark outside and the sound was ominous, scaring everyone inside the house including all the kitties and doggies put safely inside, out of the rain and wind. After the thunderous crash, there was only silence, dead silence, except for the incessant howling winds of Rita.

"Everything's okay, Mom, just another fence down and a little damage to the garage, but another huge mess to clean up around here. We lucked out again," declared a wet and wind-blown Randy, coming inside the next morning after inspecting the grounds.

"But the people in Holly Beach weren't so fortunate. I just heard on that battery radio the guys gave me in Slidell that Rita leveled the town, God help those three hundred people who lived there. Let's all pray for no more hurricanes this year."

CHAPTER THIRTY-SIX

FINAL VISIT

Linda couldn't understand the reasoning, and Bobby was certain this decision was not exactly the most sensible idea she had ever entertained, but she felt driven to have a peaceful closure with Jimmy on that bloody corner in Las Vegas.

"Bobby, why, why are you going there? Are you trying to taunt whatever it is that holds your destiny? If you won't listen to common sense and insist on being stubbornly stupid, please be careful, remember, we've a wedding to attend next month, your daughter is depending on you."

"I'll be there, Sis, 'cause there's also another very important reason for being in Ohio that I haven't told you about: Ben and I getting married as soon as I get back from Vegas, after Cindy's wedding. Linda, Ben has been my special friend and mentor for years, long before John died. You know I'll always love Sid, he'll forever be tucked away in my dreams, but Ben is the one who has brought inner peace into my life, and I'm eager to spend my quiet years with him."

"Well for Pete's sake, it's about time. Your kids and I have known for years that Ben is the perfect one for you. When did all of this happen? Common', tell your little sister all about it."

"Well, right before Mom died I received a letter from him, and after you left for Florida and I was still in Ohio, we got together and had a long talk. He just wouldn't take no or maybe for an answer, telling me that Sid's instructions before he died told him to take care of me. He told me it was common knowledge that Sid always got what Sid wanted, and he was going to see that Sid's last wish was fulfilled."

Then he told me, "Bobby, I'm going to be with you even if it means all I can do is put my shoes under your bed."

"Well, what else could I do? You know how I feel about washing a man's socks without being in his will, so I said 'yes'."

"Bobby, you are a real trip. Take special care settling up those old issues in Vegas and get back here and enjoy that man, he deserves it—and so do you, Sis."

Michael was at his concierge desk lining up guest requests when he happened to glance through the Flamingo glass doors to Las Vegas Boulevard when he saw her.

It had been years, although there were always a couple busboys ready to repeat the rumor they actually spotted her there once or twice, he hadn't actually seen her for years, until today. He wished old Gus were still here—Gus's red-headed lady had become as infamous at the Flamingo as that mysterious, dark-robed ghostly woman who appeared yearly to haunt Valentino's grave.

She was there, on the sidewalk between the Flamingo and Barbary Coast Casinos, with the sun streaming through her hair creating an illusion of a red halo, standing on that exact spot where he and Gus witnessed her many angry tirades against God, or someone, or something. The stories varied depending on who was doing the telling.

Old Gus died several years ago, and Michael assumed the red-headed lady was gone also, but there she stood, with a red crown shining around her head, just as petite as she was that day he had lost the twenty bucks bet to Gus.

Feeling an urgent curiosity, he layed down the paper requests, and then took a few steps, positioning himself nearer the front door so he could get a closer look at Gus's lady. He immediately recognized she was more relaxed as she stood there, more serene than he remembered.

Then she looked up at the sky and he saw her make the sign of the cross. She looked at peace with the world and he knew she was praying.

As Michael turned and walked slowly back to his concierge area, he fervently hoped God heard prayers from the sidewalk in front of the Flamingo on Las Vegas Boulevard.

Old Gus would have liked this day.

CHAPTER THIRTY-SEVEN

THE END?

It was close to midnight in Ohio when Cindy, fast asleep, realized the phone was ringing. Who would be calling at this time of night, certainly couldn't be good news. Groping in the dark, she reached over to the nightstand, turned on the light, and answered the impatient telephone.

"Hello?"

"Sis, there's no good way to tell you this. The plane crashed, it went down, the news came over CNN about a half hour ago and the airline just called me," he choked up, then continued, "Cindy, Mom was on that plane, coming back from Vegas, and it went down in the swamp on the way into New Orleans. CNN reports there are only a few surviv…"

"Oh, my God!" she interrupted, "I pray one of them is Mother. First Daddy getting murdered in Vegas, now Mother dead, traveling from there? You know, she mentioned something about their destiny with Las Vegas, but I just didn't listen closely enough, Randy. I always considered that it was religious gibberish, something like the Myers' Curse claims. Please, Randy, call me just as soon as you hear something."

Cindy sat for what seemed like an eternity waiting for the phone to ring again.

It didn't.

She waited and waited.

The grin slowly covered her pretty round face, a face still child-like despite being middle-aged. It was a grin that spread out like the wings of one of those little yellow field butterflies as they unfold atop a perfect rose. An observer would say her mother had picked the perfect nickname for her.

Cindy Butterfly knew. She knew in her heart. Mother had promised to be at her wedding, and Cindy knew Mother would be there, one way or another. She had never broken a promise to Cindy.

"Thank you God," she murmured as she reached up and turned off the light.